The Invite

C.P. RICHES

ISBN: 9798760399144

CONTENTS

ACKNOWLEDGMENTS

I would like to offer special thanks to Sue Gerrard and Amy Banks for their invaluable editorial input and encouragement. I want to also thank my fiancé Jenny for your continual support and patience and also for being the editor I didn't know I needed. Also, to family and friends; without your kind words and motivation, the end result wouldn't have been possible.

1

THE INVITATION

One swift swipe of the finger and a welcoming glow absorbed my eyes. The sudden rush of vibrant colours was an exciting overload that drowned out the howling wind and extinguished the dreary grey depression of outside.

Sweat-smeared windows had confined me to a stuffy nightmare in which I was squashed like a tinned sardine. Frequent eruptions of unjustified laughter and poor behaviour had already made me feel angry inside, even though I knew the journey would not be a long one.

I hated the school bus. In fact, I just hated school in general. Everything about the place made me feel depressed.

My name is Lindsey Hoodwink. I am an average-looking 16-year-old girl, with average grades, in a school full of know-it-all snobs and delinquents. Life was a such a drag, and today was just another battle.

I was sat alone praying that no pimply-faced little freak would sit down and pester me. I had to hold out for two more stops before we reached my bestie's stop and sanctuary was guaranteed. Fortunately, I was able to drown out the repetitive torture of the trip by staying glued to the gift of endless opportunity that is my smartphone.

A world of wonders awaited as the beautiful beam of my phone screen hit me. It made me feel like a kid in a sweetshop trying to decide on her favourite sugary treat. It didn't take me long to initiate the choice of familiarity, but upon making the decision I knew it would make me feel great. And it did. A constant scrolling on the screen followed and time was sucked away like a hoover working at full suction.

We were soon at Sammy's stop. I didn't need to work for her attention. I had taken up pretty much two seats and we always sat in the same place. I heard a muffled, 'Hey Linds,' which signalled me to shift in order for her to shield me from getting stuck sat next to a tragic case. I was too engrossed in a stream of comments about gender neutrality to deter myself from the screen at that moment to greet Sammy with conversation as she sat down.

Out of the corner of my eye I could see Sammy had received the memo that I wanted peace and was soon swiping away on her new smartphone rather than chomping my ear off at this early hour. Sammy's new phone was so sleek in comparison to mine. Mine was on point when it first came out but compared to hers it was a relic. It made my blood boil to think I was at a disadvantage for being the first to be cutting edge.

Don't get me wrong, I loved Sammy to bits, but she carried herself with an air of perfection that I could never achieve. I could never attain her killer curves, grow boobs like bowling balls and radiate flawless skin like hers. Instead I had gangly, stick-like legs, rugged skin and dull blonde hair that I pulled back in a bun every day because I couldn't get up early enough in the morning to make a decent job of it.

Having motored through a mass of apps already, which included a variety of mind-numbing games and pretty much every form of social media you can imagine, I suddenly succumbed to feelings of outrage.

'Look at this, Amy's just posted!' I exclaimed, shocked at what I had just unearthed.

'What is she going on about this time?' Sammy replied, amused at my discovery.

'God, she sounds so desperate, it makes me cringe,' I continued.

The pouting pose of Amy lit up my screen and invaded my space. #Badhairday was the caption, even though her hair looked as straight as a ruler. The tightly-squeezed tit package that was bulging through the screen was evidently the real reason for the post.

Ridiculous people were making me angry. I should have really switched my attention to my friend, but then suddenly the Balloon Trouble game caught my eye. Just one go before we have a gossip, I thought. I was so close to cracking this level. I just needed to deliver one more pinpoint shot at the yellow balloon with my spear and victory would be sweet.

We had soon bypassed both Sammy's estate and the stretch of saturated Cheshire countryside that followed, after which the school bus came to an abrupt halt. My wretched school, Halden High, was the final destination and almost everyone exited like a pack of hungry dogs. On the other hand I was in no rush at all and daydreamed steadily towards the school grounds; eyes still glued rigidly to my screen.

'See you then,' said Sammy before filtering away with a glum-looking expression on her face.

I think I acknowledged with a slight wave; my nose remaining buried in the balloon carnage.

Barely realising, I had somehow made it into my perfectly square maths room, which was humid and uncomfortable, and I was assaulted with artificial light that stung my eyes. After reluctantly slipping my phone into my blazer top pocket for easy access, my stinging eyes were further hindered as they tried to adjust to a bigger screen. The fact it seemed quite blurry even though I was perched stupidly close, suggested that poor eyesight was becoming just another one of my many life problems.

Mr Walters had already started the lesson. I must have arrived ridiculously late again. I quickly opened my GCSE revision book to a clean page. Exams were only a few months away and I was determined not to get distracted again. Maths was proving to be somewhat of a challenge!

'Right class, we are now going to revisit trigonometry,' said Mr Walters, which was greeted by a sea of groans.

Oh great, trigonometry! You can do this, I thought. I just

needed to focus and practice the examples. I knew I was kidding myself with the enthusiasm. I'd been trying to understand this nasty little beast for weeks now. I even created dedicated post it notes and stuck them on the back of my phone to look at whenever I needed them. In all fairness I don't think I've actually referred back at the notes as yet. I keep meaning to, but then somehow always get distracted by notifications that need to be dealt with. I did make an attempt to one time, but ended up completely zoning out and drew mindless doodles on the notes instead. I mean who on earth needs Trigonometry in the real world anyway? What a waste of time.

'As I said previously, trigonometry can be used to calculate the lengths of sides and sizes of angles in right-angled triangles. The main thing to remember is the three formulae: sin, cos and tan,' Mr Walters continued.

Ok got that, my inner optimist chorused with encouragement.

Mr Walters continued his breakdown of the beast and with each step I was gaining confidence in my understanding; but then suddenly a series of quick-fire vibrations went off like a loaded gun in my blazer pocket, and I completely lost my train of thought. An overwhelming urge gripped me, and I longed to uncover the cause. No, I must resist, I told myself. Whatever it is, it can wait. I've almost cracked this.

But then another voice drowned out the voice of reason. What if it's important, an emergency even? Even if it isn't, shouldn't I just check and make sure? It will only take two secs and then I can fully focus back on mastering this.

In one swift movement, I removed the phone from my pocket and buried my hands beneath the desk. Mr Walters never suspected a thing.

The drab underbelly of my desk was suddenly illuminated, and my screen indicated that I had two emails and one notification. I knew the emails were probably junk and so I tapped on the notification first.

Annoyingly it was a pointless one. You have been sent a

request to join Virtuality, it read. The rage bubbled inside me at the thought of being distracted by spam. I may well have dwelt a little more on the obscure request if it wasn't for the push message that just invaded my screen. It was from Jade Bowen, the queen bee of Halden High who announced she was having a party this weekend and I was invited!

I must admit I disliked the girl, but I was still buzzing. Anyone who was anyone would be attending. This would surely include Brad, I thought with excitement. Brad happened to be one of the fittest lads in the year! We had been messaging for the past few weeks after enduring a painful hour-long detention together for misbehaving in maths class. We somehow got chatting; or rather, messing around. He has been a total flirt since we started talking and I'm convinced that Jade's party would be an epic opportunity to get in there.

Even though I wanted to play it cool, I couldn't resist replying to confirm my attendance. At this point, all thoughts of maths had washed away, and I spent the rest of the lesson being dragged in by waves of messages from others who were also thrilled over their invites.

It was only when Mr Walter's booming voice echoed in my direction, did I break contact with my screen. The disturbance really angered me.

'Earth to Lindsey! I've been watching you for the past ten minutes playing on your phone under the desk. Is there something really important you would like to share with the group?'

The classroom occupants howled childishly along to Mr Walters' sarcastic remarks. He really does think he's funny. Annoyingly, I had no leg to stand on and clearly didn't wish to share the content of my messages with the classroom. This was the intention of course, and it just wound me up even more. I felt like being a smart-ass back but thought better of it.

'I was just checking something out sir,' I responded.

'I see, and that takes ten minutes does it?' he fired back at me.

I could feel myself going ruby red with anger and embarrassment.

'Obviously not, sir.'

It was clear I had gone too far with my sassy reply and Mr Walters was seething.

'Is that so? Well that means you were obviously not paying attention to the lesson, I presume. You were obviously breaking the rules about using phones during lesson time.'

I couldn't tell if he was trying to catch me out with sarky questions or was merely stating the filthy truth and so I just found myself shrugging at him. This was clearly enough to tip Mr Walters over the edge.

'This is the fourth time this week I've had to tell you about using your phone in my lesson and I won't stand for it. GCSEs are getting ever closer and you need to be making the best use of what little time you have left in these lessons.'

'Please leave the classroom and seriously reflect on how you should be spending your time in our final lessons. I will be speaking with your head of year in due course about this.'

I felt a surge of humiliation and regret as I endured the walk of shame out of the classroom. The drama promptly muted the previously giddy classroom, which made things more awkward as I left. Laden with guilt for my actions, I found myself doing laps around school in the ten-minute wait for my next lesson to start. I knew I had to get my act together in order to succeed. I was dead set on going to college and actually getting somewhere in life but couldn't wait to leave school and do things my own way for a change. I had no real clue about what I wanted to do with my life to be honest; I just knew I wanted to be my own boss and make a success for myself like my dad.

My vision for a bright future seemed like a passing pipe dream to be honest and after just one lap of walking the school grounds I couldn't help but bury my nose back in my phone again to fixate on the continuing party messages that peppered me with notifications. At least I could do so in peace now.

The party messages continued to flood in throughout the day and what had at first started off as excitement (even if it did get me in the shit), soon became an irritation. On the way home, it was obvious that my phone was exhausted due to the constant buzz of eager messages. It had a temperature and its battery was about to die. Luckily, I just had enough power to get me through one final game of Balloon Trouble.

I was in such a good mood when I got home. The rain had finally cleared, and the last light of the day shone brightly through my bedroom window, warming me nicely. I still felt a little cocky from the earlier invite and couldn't resist messaging Sammy some more about it. Looking back, that was a bit insensitive of me as she hadn't been invited. I must say she seemed happy for me, nonetheless.

What a great week this was looking to be. There was just one little hurdle to overcome and then the rest would be plain sailing. I needed to persuade the parents to let me attend the party somehow and had a cunning plan of action to win them over, which involved some serious buttering up. I had to master my scheme to perfection, and I knew I had to act quickly.

2

THE PLAN

Come the following day, I had formulated a foolproof plan to win over my parent's approval to attend the party. I had already initiated phase one; this involved undertaking the morning brew round. Phase two would consist of helping with dinner preparation. After this, the final step would include an offer to do the washing up before taking the plunge and praying for a result.

It was Wednesday already, so if all else failed I would have two days to unleash a tantrum to end all tantrums in pursuit of my goal.

After the distractions of the previous day, I found it even harder to concentrate at school. Even in English, a subject that I thrived in and always found engaging, I just couldn't keep it together. Dreams of success in my master plan immersed me and my phone was also like a magnet that sucked me in, as the party message stream from yesterday gushed on and on.

I met up with Sammy at lunch time and was grateful for her presence, so I could run my scheme by her.

'Wow, you do have this all figured out, don't you?' Sammy questioned, looking impressed.

I couldn't tell if her tone was that of mockery, but nonetheless she seemed interested. That was good enough for me.

'Yeah, I know, I just really wanna go. All I ever do is work these days. Be good to actually have some fun for a change, plus Brad's bound to be going.'

It was true that I seemed to do nothing but work lately; not only did I have constant revision crammed down my throat every night, but I also had little freedom on the weekends. Every Friday and Saturday night I had to slave away until the early hours collecting grim empty pint glasses from pervy old men in the working men's club down the road. But not this weekend. This weekend was a rare weekend off and I fully intended to make the most of it! I couldn't help but notice Sammy was looking surprised and also a little deflated at my last comment.

It suddenly dawned on me that Sammy still hadn't received an invite and I was probably being a bit insensitive again. Feeling awful about the situation, I decided to drop it.

I instinctively reached for my phone and discovered a notification to say it was my cousin Katie's birthday. She was two years older than me and much prettier. What's more, she seemed to have life all figured out, which made me feel like a bit of a failure. Clearly the one who had been blessed with the family brains, she was studying science at college and to top it off, had a fit older boyfriend (or should I say fiancé) called Craig who was at uni? At least I was an only child and didn't have to compete with high-achieving siblings too.

After wishing her happy birthday on her page, I couldn't help but notice she had posted videos with her boyfriend at a theme park somewhere that looked exotic. They seemed to be having a right laugh. It was nosy I know, but after invading the first I couldn't help but notice others she had posted. Each video filled me with both joy and sadness for some reason.

I was finally distracted by Sammy who informed me that she was off to her next class. At first, I thought she was being rude but then realised that I was running late for my next lesson.

The afternoon passed in a blink of an eye and by the time I was on the bus home, I was confident I would nail my parent's approval for the weekend.

As soon as I got through the front door, I quickly changed and swooped into action peeling and chopping potatoes. I had planned ahead and already messaged my mum to announce my great gesture to come.

I was left in peace for a good ten minutes before anyone came home. I absent-mindedly watched a bird foraging in the garden. I did love the view out of the kitchen window. It consisted of a long luscious lawn cordoned off by grand oak trees. The view was like a panoramic postcard where the landscape forced its way through the trees. Inside the house was pretty nice too. I was cooking in a stylish new kitchen and everything else screamed of expense.

I had almost forgotten about the task in hand; but then my mum came in. Contrary to her text back, it quickly became clear that she detected a rat.

'So, what's all this in aid of then?' she demanded. 'Is that Lindsey, actually offering to help around the house? You must be after something? Go on, what is it?'

My mum was nobody's fool. It was naive of me to think this would be a walk in the park. I knew I had to play it cool.

'Nothing, just thought I would help out for a change,' I casually replied. 'Plus, I'm starving and didn't want to wait for hours to eat.'

My mum did not look convinced, but it seemed to appease her for now.

We spent the next half an hour preparing tea and talking girl trash, all the while I aggressively plotted and schemed. I knew my dad would have the final say and so I had to face the bull head on. Dad arrived home shortly after and was miraculously in a good mood. This was a rare occurrence and something I intended to exploit. It was time to cast the bait. However, I couldn't figure out a way to broach the subject. Words eluded me. I decided to go upstairs and change in order to finalise my plan of action.

As I left the sanctuary of my room to finish the deed, I suddenly got riddled with nerves. I knew if my parents wouldn't play ball, that would be the end of that. I would be the dull girl who was too sensible for parties. I would be cast aside with all the other average Joe's. I probably wouldn't get invited to a party again.

After each step downstairs, my heart picked up pace. My hands were clammy and my throat dry. This was ridiculous. The dining room drew ever nearer. As I approached the final door of destiny, I took a deep breath, and then sailed straight into the heart of the storm.

3

HEART OF THE STORM

My mum was preparing to serve tea as I entered the room and luckily my dad was sat in the front room. This eased the tension somewhat, but I knew the delay would just intensify the task. I considered just targeting my mum first, but I knew that was the cowardly approach. Moreover, I knew she would just run things past my dad anyway, so it was no use. I sat down and awaited my fate.

'Tea's ready,' my mum shouted.

My dad sat at the top of the dining room table, my mum at the other end, with me trapped in the middle.

'What a day!' my dad declared with delight. 'Got the keys to the new barge this morning.'

Here we go, I thought. Dad had done nothing but harp on about this new bloody canal boat he had bought. Dad bought tatty old boats for a living, renovated them, and then rented them out for parties and day experiences in the popular Cheshire waterways. I wouldn't mind, but I rarely ever got to go down to see, let alone take a ride on the boats! It really irritated me how he was so obsessed with work, but this news meant he would surely be in a good mood, which offered me an injection of hope!

'That's great news,' my mum replied. 'We should go out at the weekend and celebrate.'

I knew this proposition would give me a window to pose the killer question, but I didn't like where the conversation was now heading.

'Yeah, why not?' replied my dad with too much enthusiasm for my liking. I knew what was coming.

'What do you reckon, Linds, do you fancy coming out with us on Saturday to celebrate seeing as you're not working?' questioned my mum.

Shit. This is definitely not how I wanted this conversation to go. Here goes nothing. 'Well I was thinking of going to Jade's on Saturday night. She's invited a couple of the girls to stay over and watch a film and that.' As I uttered the words, it was obvious that I reeked of insincerity. I suddenly realised how lame my white lie sounded.

As expected, my dad reacted like Mr Hyde. 'Oh, it's all coming out now, isn't it? This is why she was helping out making the tea, Louise.' Undertones of rage in his voice intensified as he continued to rant.

'You're right, Greg, I knew there was a hidden agenda. You don't even like that Jade girl,' mum remarked, suddenly reverting back to me.

I immediately unleashed the force field. 'When did I say that? Me and Jade have always got on. Besides, Sammy's going, and it's been ages since we've done anything with all this revising.'

This move was quickly deflected by the unforgiving parents who fed off each other like a pack of wolves surrounding their prey.

'I thought Sammy didn't like Jade either?' my mum probed.

'Yeah, you were telling us the other week how Jade always ignored her and bitched about her online,' my dad added.

God, why did my dad have to be so observant. He was like Columbo or something. I was walking in quicksand and sinking fast. It was a code red. Time to unleash the drama queen if things didn't take a miraculous turn.

'Yeah, they just had a bit of a thing. They are cool now.'

Neither parent looked convinced.

'I think you're full of it, Linds. You're not going and that's the end of it!' shouted my dad, with an air of finality.

'God, you're so unfair!' I shot back. 'I can't do anything! I'm not a child, you know.'

I could see my dad boiling over. As expected, a war had quickly imploded, 'when you're in my house, you're under my rules. Don't think I've forgot what happened last time!'

It was really quite hard to argue with that last point. A few months ago, I convinced my parents to let me sleep over at Sammy's when in fact I sneaked out to a house party. My mum tried calling me to let me know that I had forgotten my toothbrush; however, in my drunken state I missed the call and she only went ahead and called Sammy's mum who was utterly bewildered and annoyed at my deceit. This was nothing compared to the rage I endured thereafter. My mum called again and again and left me a string of scary messages, demanded I came home right now. I dared not ignore them and suffered the consequences as I returned back in a drunken state. Why did I have to get myself into these situations?

Now that I had all but lost the battle, the defeat started to act like a fuel that was igniting an uncompromising rage within me.

'God, give me a break. I made one mistake and now you're treating me like a prisoner. All my other friends can go to their friends' at the weekend and I always have to be the loser who misses out. I hate my life!'

Overwhelmed with fury, I stormed out of the dining room, red-faced and shaking uncontrollably. I flew up the stairs, into my room and slammed the door behind me, leaving my half-eaten tea abandoned indefinitely.

I felt unhinged and needed some solitude to restore my inner peace. Luckily, my phone sat innocently on the side, waiting to be my saving grace. I instinctively went to access social media but then the thought of more party messages hit me like a dagger cutting deep into my soul. Instead, I opened a music playlist that was tailormade for this exact mood. It was first filled with rock songs which helped empty the tank of insatiable anger and then switched to heart-breaking love songs which helped satisfy the deep depressive mood which would inevitably come. I curled up into a ball, cradling my phone and refused to move for anybody until school the next day.

4

THE AFTERMATH

Surprisingly, I slept well after the fight. I must have burned myself out. The reality of the end result slapped me hard in the face again the next day though and riddled me with a poisonous mood that tore through everything that crossed my path.

Regrettably, Sammy was soon in the firing line. It was god-awful timing considering the unjustified ill treatment I had been serving her lately. 'How can they treat me like this?' I demanded as my rant hit full throttle on the morning bus ride. 'They are such pricks. They never let me do anything.'

Although she tried to look empathetic, I could detect an underlying smugness as she tried to console me. I can't say I blamed her, but it angered me, nonetheless. 'Why wouldn't they let you go?' she asked.

'Oh, just the same old shit. My dad went all dictator again on me, going on about what happened last time. My mum kept having digs as well saying that I didn't even like Jade.'

I could tell Sammy wanted to agree that Jade and I were not close, but she didn't. 'Yeah, that does suck,' she offered, seemingly struggling for a more meaningful response. 'At least you got invited though,' she added, clearly unable to help herself.

I felt a surge of guilt which added to the temper, making me feel utterly lousy. I knew a good friend would be comforting at that moment, and so through gritted teeth I tried to be just that, even if the response was not altogether heartfelt.

'Yeah, well, it will probably be crap anyway now that we are not going,' I said, confident that this would remedy Sammy's ill feelings and who knows, hopefully mine too. It seemed to help take the edge off.

'Yeah, you're right, Linds. How about we do something on Saturday instead?'

Surprisingly, the invite made me feel slightly better and so I accepted the offer. We spent the remainder of the bus journey bitching about parents and Jade. The rant was quite therapeutic, and I barely gave the situation another thought for the rest of the day.

I almost felt in a good mood, that is until I made it back home that evening. The thought of facing my parents again instantly reignited last night's flames. I decided that the war was still not over and made a conscious effort to avoid them that night. I would often have a nice girly chat with my mum after school and we would both rant about the day. Not today! I darted straight upstairs and into my room. I thought this decision would empower me, but I somehow felt worse in the confinement of four walls.

Luckily, I had my phone at hand as an escape. The welcoming warmth of my beach background greeted me when I swiped open the home screen. It was an idyllic image of a secluded beach in Thailand. The scene boasted crystal clear water, chalk-like sand and delightful greenery that poked out of the sea like magic. I'd never been there of course, but how I would love to go. My cousin Katie was there with her fiancé, Craig. They were travelling across East Asia and having the time of their lives I bet. I wish I could have clicked my fingers and be transported there in an instant, far away from this miserable existence. The only thing ruining the perfect scene was a big spidery crack that had infested the corner of the screen. I had achieved this after only a week of having the phone. I dropped it whilst trying to take a selfie in the bathroom resulting in a nice big smash as it collided with the solid floor tiles. What an idiot.

Frustratingly, my phone charge status signalled bad news.

It needed life support again. I had no choice but to use it whilst it was plugged in on charge. Stupid battery life was a nightmare.

I was about to conquer the latest level on my Balloon Trouble game. I had come so close last time but failed at the final hurdle. This time I was determined. I don't know what it was about this game. It was unbelievably stress-inducing trying to figure out where to throw the vibrantly coloured spears, only to fail time and time again; but each failure dictated that I take another go. It also annoyed me how unrealistically happy my cartoon warrior character looked as he launched the spears into the web of confusion. My commander's Roman-style armour along with his daft-looking sandals and long, jet-black hair did little but add further irritation to his constant cheesy grin.

I failed once, twice, three times, and was starting to get irritated. At that moment, I heard my mum heading to my room. I knew she could sense the ill feelings were still rife. I also knew that she would have erased any anger from last night and would want to make amends. Fat chance of that happening. Sure enough, there was a subtle knock on my door. I chose to ignore it.

'Are you in there Lindsey?' my mum questioned, even though she quite clearly knew I was.

'Yeah, what do you want?'

'I was just seeing what you wanted for tea,' she replied with warmth, in contrast to my stone-cold tone.

'I don't want any,' I lied. I was quite hungry but was determined not to let them win.

My mum then entered the room, uninvited and tried to appeal to my better nature. 'Stop being so silly,' she pleaded. 'Why don't you and Sammy go and do something instead? I don't care what you say, I could bet this house that she won't be able to go the party either.'

God, I hated how she was always right. I swear she could read minds. I refused to declare that I had already taken her expert advice though.

'Or you could head out with us like your dad said. We'll have a nice slap-up meal, and we might even let you have a cheeky wine.'

Every word she spoke caused the anger inside to bubble up like a simmering volcano. It was a force of nature. I was too exhausted to start another World War though and so just gritted my teeth and appeased her.

'Yeah, I might do.'

This seemed enough to satisfy her for now.

'Ok. It will be a laugh anyway,' my mum concluded before probing me again. 'What do you want for tea then?'

I was sticking to my guns on this one. I didn't want her to think they had won so easily.

'Nothing, I'm not hungry,' I said.

I knew this ground on my mum's nerves, but she tried not to show it.

'Fine, but make sure you eat something before bed,' she pleaded.

Thankfully, she left me in peace after her final plea. I did intend to eat, but I had no intention of leaving my room. Annoyingly, I only had a slightly crushed bag of crisps as immediate fuel. It would have to do.

It wasn't long before the hunger hit me again and it only added to my depressive state. I failed multiple attempts on Balloon Trouble and so spent an endless amount of time scrolling through friends' updates. I don't know what I was in search of, but whatever it was, I could not find it and got annoyed.

I decided to cast my phone aside and watch some trash TV instead. This obviously failed to engage me and before I knew it, I was absent-mindedly scrolling again. Luckily there had been no party messages today, but this annoyed me a little for some reason. It felt as though the planned events were final and this just reminded me that I was no longer a part of them.

5

THE BACK-UP PLAN

The next day, messages came through like rapid fire and it felt like I was the target. Everyone was so excited about the party it was unreal. Jade kept boasting about what she was going to wear, whilst others kissed her ass about it. Some plotted ways in which they would sneak in booze whilst others talked about the banging playlists they had created for the occasion. Aside from my bitterness towards the whole thing, what angered me more is that my phone couldn't handle the heat and was on its deathbed by mid-day. I swear if I don't get a new phone soon, I'm going to have a breakdown.

By mid-afternoon everyone seemed joyous; evidently blinded by the promise of a weekend break. The feeling was not mutual. Even the easy ICT class which concluded the week couldn't ease my anger. It was literally the only subject I enjoyed and was actually good at (well besides English I suppose), but it was ruined by a clan of Jade's besties boasting about their brilliant weekend ahead. A wicked vision that depicted me launching one of the water laden balloons from my favourite game at them, suddenly invaded my thoughts.

The end-of-week bell was a welcoming screech which prompted me to exit school like a lava eruption. I felt suffocated by everyone else's smugness.

Unable to endure the unruly chaos of a bus ride, I decided to walk home, even though it was a good 45-minute walk. I ate up ground with blistering pace and was halfway home before remembering that I was meant to wait for Sammy after school.

The shitty friend strikes again.

I made it home much quicker than anticipated and even though the walk had been a detox, my mood immediately became murky as I entered the weekend cell. As soon as I got inside, I placed my phone into revival mode and waited for it to breathe again. I had felt lost without it that afternoon.

Sure enough, both parents were soon home, and both seemed in high spirits like everyone else. It made me want to hurl. I ignored both of them and stormed straight up to my room.

As anticipated, my mum shouted me down for food at six. I couldn't cope with another night of starvation, so swallowed my pride and reluctantly left my room. I took my time though to ensure as little time as possible was shared with the prison guards.

I adopted the silent treatment as I ate dinner, and again, as expected, my parents probed to see what the problem was, even though they knew damn well.

'Why do you have a face on again?' questioned mum.

'Yeah, it's Friday, what's up with you?' my dad further interrogated.

'Nothing,' I replied.

Neither parent seemed convinced and they continued to grill me until the opportunity to escape presented itself.

I spent the remainder of the night attacking games on my phone. I had downloaded some rather addictive real-life game called A Mogul's Empire where I had to build my own business from scratch. For about an hour or so, I was released from my shackles.

The relentless game bashing cleared my mind and I slept like a log. I was determined not to be corrupted by jealous thoughts and bitterness, so figured the only solution was distraction. I decided to organise a jam-packed schedule to keep me productive and more importantly to keep my mind off last night's hellish results. It was now clear that I had failed in my mission to win over the parents and I failed in my follow-up to make them feel guilty. To top it all off, I had failed over and over again to complete that wretched level on Balloon Trouble and so I decided it was time to move on and distract myself in other ways.

I started out with a jog around the village. It was a glorious morning. The sluggish spring was at last starting to awake from hibernation and it provided me with a much-needed boost to deflect my stormy mood. As I meandered steadily on for a good while my thoughts were occupied with little more than the pretty houses I encountered and the leafy paths which offered pristine views of sun-absorbed fields.

Annoyingly, I had to stop before too long as a savage stitch ripped into my chest, reminding me of just how unfit I was. I was puffing like a steam train and glistened in sweat. My body literally forced me to stop and I decided to walk the rest of the way back.

Even though I didn't run the whole way, I still rewarded myself with a cup of tea and contradictory cake for my morning efforts. This was followed by a period of self-loathing for ruining the diet before I forced my attention back to the next task.

I worked through all the necessary revision, tidied my room, had lunch and then had a shower; all without a care in the world. I felt accomplished by the time I was finished. I no longer felt sluggish and bitter; dare I say I was beginning to actually look forward to the rest of the weekend? However, I had a quick look at the clock and it just laughed at me. It was only 2pm and I had exhausted all ammunition to distract me from thinking about the party. Although it was ridiculous, I suddenly sensed a black cloud could swamp me at any moment and I was determined not to fall into a foul mood again.

Luckily, I had a light bulb moment. I would text Sammy and see if she wanted me round early. This way I would no longer be bored, Sammy would take this as an apology for my narky mood and I could even have an early drink to help further deflect any thoughts of tonight. Everyone wins.

I sent Sammy a nice inviting message and awaited eagerly for her response. Remarkably, I actually felt excitement as I waited for her to accept my offer. A problem I did not anticipate however, is that acceptance was not forthcoming. In fact, I failed to get any response. Sammy usually texted back straight away, but now a good thirty minutes had passed and still nothing.

Sure enough, my excitement began to disappear and instead anger and paranoia took its place. How dare she ignore me! What if she's really upset with me over yesterday? What if she's been invited to the party after all? My head was spinning with ill thoughts.

It was over an hour and half until I got a response, which simply said, 'Yeah, come round wenever x.'

This should have solved all issues, but it didn't. I read the message over and over and with each turn I was left feeling increasingly more outraged. She was clearly being sassy and didn't want me to come round. I decided to ignore her and instead reach for my only friend in the world.

6

THE SMART PHONE

I instantly felt better for grabbing my phone. I was liked a stressed-out smoker reaching for a cigarette. Habitually, my fingers directed me to social media, but I recoiled, knowing it would only lure me into a trap of the night's endeavours to come. Instead I returned to my Balloon Trouble quest, which I smashed through with great satisfaction. However as soon as I hit level 252 the anger of constant failure started to kick in and so I ended the game and moved back onto A Mogul's Empire. I had already set up my own offices and was able to create the buildings, style the interiors and purchase essential gear such as desks, PC's and phones. It was so realistic I actually felt like a real-life business nut. My next task was to arrange interviews from a selection of candidates that had already applied to work for my company. Trying to choose the best CV's was a bit of a brain tease.

As I became rapidly absorbed in the game, the boundaries of time became blurred. I must have been on the game for hours and only vaguely heard the muffled voice of my mum shouting to me from the top of the stairs. A part of me purposely chose to ignore her call. Regardless of this, I felt like my brain had suddenly turned to melting butter and I didn't have the instruction to respond, even if I wanted to.

My eyes were wide open, glued to a tiny screen. 100% of my brain was focussed on the phone. Someone could have punched me and I wouldn't have felt a thing. The minutes flew by and I had no power to slow them as I lay shackled to my best friend.

This daze was abruptly broken by a notification which intruded onto the screen. For some strange reason, it infuriated me, as if I had been rudely awoken from an idyllic dream; stripped of all euphoria. Moreover, a feeling of weightlessness, I never knew I had, was now wearing off and I was suddenly reintroduced to my senses. I was crashing back to earth.

Virtuality has sent you an invite.

I immediately recognised the name, as it was identical to the notification I received only a few days earlier. I initially thought this was one of those irritating spam notifications that you get on social media, but this time the notification had pinged straight onto my home screen; there was no evidence as to where it came from. It didn't immediately look like an app; in fact, I wasn't sure what it was.

This time I was intrigued. In fact, it was more than that. Curiosity spread through me like wildfire. I was gripped by a commanding urge and my finger felt like a powerful magnet that was being thrust into a large metal plate.

I clicked the large, circular, emerald green button in the middle of the screen, which pleaded, 'Begin your journey'.

At first, nothing happened. What a waste of time, I thought.

A loading bar, however, soon appeared on screen. It was clear this was going to take an eternity to load as a small blue slither ebbed its way into the corner of the bar. Even though it was obvious the load would take forever, I couldn't help but observe its progress and a feeling of hypnosis was starting to kidnap me again.

Each slight nudge towards completion made my eyes roll. In fact, my eyes were being hoodwinked as the loading bar suddenly seemed to have grown remarkably in size. It now occupied around two inches of the screen rather than a measly half centimetre, but it was growing by the second. It looked like a limp balloon that was suddenly pumped with air.

Soon it was squashed in the corner of the screen, screaming to get out. Then, remarkably, the glass on my phone shattered into a thousand pieces and it erupted out of the phone. The loading bar was now an occupant of my room and floated ominously just above my bed, letting off a slight buzz, like a computer on charge.

I just sat there on my bed, in a trance, unable to comprehend what had just happened. Any normal person would have given their head a shake or run for the hills, but all I could do was sit and stare.

At that point, the loading bar stopped growing in size, but blue progress continued to flow towards completion. The loading bar stopped with a little over a third to go and then all sound on earth was muted. I immediately thought I had gone deaf. I have no idea why, but I wasn't worried by it. I had fallen into a sleep-like state where nothing seemed to matter at that moment.

For a split second, I allowed my eyes to escape from the screen. In any normal state of mind, I would have wished I hadn't. Everything had become out of focus. It was as though someone was gluing thick panes of inappropriate lenses over my eyes and demanded that they stay there.

Then everything turned pixelated. My sleek, straight, white bed covers had amazingly turned into an object made up of millions of tiny squares, each a slightly different shade of cream, white or black shadow. An indescribable awe embraced me. I longed to find out more about the transformation, but when I reached out to touch the bed duvet, I felt nothing but air.

I looked around only to find my entire room was an image, completely distorted by a tsunami of pixels. My TV looked like a sickening swamp of unnaturally-shaped fish eggs. The sky outside my window was saturated by an array of colours that twinkled in the late afternoon sun.

In the sheer astonishment at what was unfolding, it took me far too long to notice that I was in fact pixelated also. What's more, I was also a massless individual. A touch of my digitalised skin confirmed that there was more density in the wind, as my hand slipped straight through my body. This was impossible.

What on earth was my brain conjuring up? Had I really given myself square eyes? Perhaps I'd had a caffeine overload? How come I couldn't feel my body? Had I randomly fallen asleep and this was some kind of freaky dream?

Things were about to get even more bizarre. The items that were pixelated now spontaneously started to disappear. Some invisible force was wiping away my room, kind of how I erase my useless answers in maths exams.

Somewhere inside my stuffy head, fear hit me as I waited to be washed away like the cluster of scattered pixels that had now replaced my room. Before I had a chance to consider the thought of being swallowed up along with my room and enduring whatever grave ending potentially awaited however, I started to become more refined. The pixels were rapidly sharpening up. My slightly fake-tanned skin was becoming more vibrant. More so than in reality. It shimmered like liquid caramel in blinding sun. My usual dull blonde hair was an illumination of intense bright gold and yellows.

In a state of shock, I assessed every part of me. Although unharmed, this action confirmed something sinister. I was still no longer whole. I was no longer a girl; well not a real one anyway. I felt as light as air. I was now made up of a mixture of translucent colours that shone crisply against what was now an ocean of white nothingness. I was no longer me. My hand once again slipped right through my body. I couldn't feel anything solid. I felt nothing, nothing but emptiness! What's more, with everything else eradicated, the sea of endless white seemed to be just that. Nothing else occupied this space except my sparkling, unbelievable and barely real, new self.

As I began to digest the shock of a lifetime, I decided to uproot myself from where I stood frozen still. It turned out I could still walk on what seemed to be an invisible floor. I proceeded forward in the endless space but quickly shunted by an invisible force after making it no more than just a few paces. Clearly, the infinite space that surrounded me was an illusion.

After taking a few minutes to soak up my surreal surroundings, again I was weighed down with panic. What the hell was I going to do now? It felt like an awfully long dream and even as I told myself to wake up, it had zero effect. I circled around the narrow, foreign wilderness in desperate search of something besides a blank canvas.

Time after time I chased my own tail, but it was no use. There was just nothing here. I really needed to call for help somehow. And then remarkably something appeared out of nowhere. It looked like a large curved rectangular, white button, laced with a chrome trim. It just seemed to be floating like a genie about to grant three wishes.

I had little choice but to reach out for it. A simple touch of it achieved nothing. My hand slipped straight through it. I tried again and still nothing. I was starting to get flustered. But then it occurred to me that it was a button. I therefore treated it like it was a button and gave it a push. As I did, the whole place suddenly sprung to life. Sharp yet translucent bursts of delicate violet intertwined with periwinkle blue and danced across the space, playfully bouncing off imaginary walls before settling at various obtuse angles.

Next, a huge iconic pyramid-shaped logo protruded from nowhere and marched assertively across the space before disappearing once more.

Alarm bells started to ring in my head, but I was so stunned by what I thought was happening that I refused to believe that it was. It couldn't possibly be true?

Then, without warning, mass blocks appeared in a multitude of different shapes and colours. They were all identical in size and lined up with precision that comfortably filled the space directly in front of me. A clearly titled footer accompanied each one.

This development further confirmed the wild theory of these crazy events I was quickly formulating, and this was made even more unnerving when I realised that each shape looked ... unbelievably familiar.

Images that included a map, a giant green symbolic phone and a perfectly formed yellow envelope were just a few of the daily symbols that immediately screamed out to me.

When opening and closing my eyes several times and a few pathetic attempts to slap my face, failed to release me from this fantasy, I had no choice but to conclude that I was in fact inside my smartphone; and the only logical thing that seemed left to do, was use it.

7

A NEW REALITY

I couldn't take my eyes off the incredible landscape that cast its impossible glare on me. As I looked across the magnificent screen, I was embraced by an overwhelming surge of excitement that shielded me away from any feelings of dread. In fact, I hadn't felt this giddy in years. Real excitement was hard to come by these days. I was like a kid at Christmas trying to choose which glittering gift to open first. My mouth watered at the prospect of what adventure to embark on.

It occurred to me that I couldn't feel the floor beneath my feet, but it was definitely there. A shimmering glassy reflection lay underfoot, with a gulf of white nothingness playing the part of its foundation. The stack of magnified apps floated neatly on rows identical to my phone but spanned higher than I could even reach. Aside from all of your standard icons such as the phone, text envelope and not to mention the mini-world for internet browser that were all staring me square in the face, other familiar images such as the camera, a musical note and a lined piece of paper with a dinky pencil all waited patiently. Right at the top of the phone I could make out all of the standard phone status symbols, such as a small battery, the 4 WIFI curves, but weirdly a 'No Service' message where the network symbol usually appeared. Directly below this was a giant white cloud which was accompanied with a 13°. This feature further confirmed the theory that I was inside my phone.

Somewhere on the horizon lay the vast tropical paradise that looked oh so pretty and familiar. Looking like the real thing, the perfect picture of a Thailand oasis stretched out far into the distance. In the large gaps that now occurred between each app, my background image looked so inviting. I wondered if everything here was real and I could squeeze in between and through the apps and actually get there. There was a notably large gap above the first set of standard apps, which separated all your standard stuff, such as your web browser, phone, messages, videos and camera from the slightly less important stuff, such as emails and my favourites. Hypnotised by the distant beauty ahead I longed to be a physical part of it and tried to step over and duck under the apps towards the beach. In an instant I hit an invisible shield which sent a wavelike ripple across the screen and halted me in my tracks as soon as my outstretched leg kissed the screen. It was like trying to leave a map on a computer game.

It was a shame I couldn't visit the beach of my dreams but there was little doubt from the way the screen was set out that this was my phone. Aside from the standard apps, it had all of those I downloaded, placed right where they belonged. I could not believe what I was seeing.

The familiar bubble gum pink balloon, bordered with imaginary crash lines, had quickly caught my eye whilst considering how to reach the beach as it was of course one of my favourite games and I knew full well that it was located on the second shelf of opportunity; direct in touching reach. This was so lit. Without any worry of acting foolish, I tapped on the icon and waited for what wonders awaited me next.

With that one simple tap, the background was swept away before my very eyes. This time a multitude of bright colours were being thrown across the screen and the sweet sound of carnival music filled the air. I found myself perched on what looked like a stepping-stone, which was jet black, perfectly circular and surrounded by a sea of baby blue. In the distance was a miniature looking island which was illuminated by a giant outline of a balloon. The stepping-stone on which I stood, was in fact one of many which constructed a path leading to this mystical island.

There was absolutely no doubt about it, this was the very same addictive game I bashed on a daily basis. Incredibly I was about to play Balloon Trouble, but not in a way I could have ever imagined. I knew I had to walk the path of wonder to embrace the quest ahead.

Upon my approach to the ominous island and its empty balloon, it occurred to me that this mysterious landscape was the first level marker. I vaguely remember it from that joyous day that I first discovered Balloon Trouble. Strange that I wasn't automatically transported to level 300 or whatever it was I had reached now, but that was probably for the best given this was a new and wondrous experience.

As soon as I walked towards the first outstretched branch, I was transported to a vast outline of a luscious and exotic jungle. Thick vines hung ominously from wild, green, tropical trees that sprouted large, comical looking bananas. I stood on what looked like moist ground covered with moss and wild mushrooms and I could see a fast-flowing river that gushed intently and like clockwork. My ears registered the obvious buzz of mosquitoes and a rhythmic sound of a monkey call. Then a rumble of jungle drums completed a circular soundtrack that echoed endlessly throughout the landscape. It looked as though it should have been super-hot and humid, but I felt nothing; not even the spongy ground beneath my feet offered a stimulus.

Just as I began to absorb my surroundings, a sudden thud erupted and what looked like hundreds of brightly coloured water balloons now dominated the sky over head.

I predicted what would happen next, in response to this spectacular familiarity. The brightly coloured fictitious character I regularly directed so well, would soon appear. However, as I stood, watched and waited, no such character appeared and to make matters worse the balloons seemed to be squashed so tightly together that they screeched like howling toddlers and looked like they were slipping steadily down towards me.

As I looked over again to where my saviour should have been, I noticed a giant bag with shiny sharp coloured spears poking out. This new addition confirmed my stupidity. I instinctively sprinted the short distance over to the bag and reached over to choose a spear. Just like in the game I was so used to playing, I only saw three spears in the bag; one green, one purple and one orange.

My gamer's mentality kicked in. I focussed on the water balloons immediately overhead and then those above. It was so weird actually being in the game, as I had to step back and forth to figure out the order. This is because I couldn't see the whole pattern from directly below the balloon fort.

It only took me a few moments to figure out the first move. After all, I was definitely no stranger to this game and so I went to choose my weapon, hoping to God I could pick it up. I anxiously reached into the bag and was flooded with relief when I was able to grasp and unleash the green spear. However, although I could pick it up, I felt zero sensations once more.

It was a random feeling to launch an imaginary spear, but it glided through the air with sensational speed and accuracy. The impact was exactly as I intended as it ploughed through four green water balloons. The burst balloons released a jet of water that hit the ground without causing any wet sensation as it first collided with me.

A purple spear then motored towards the front of the bag and the back one was replaced by a glistening, ruby-red one. Again, there was a straight collection of purple balloons and I felt like an Olympic athlete as my spear rifled through five of them.

Despite the unnatural, slightly disturbing and potentially harmful situation I found myself in, I was actually having fun as I continued to pierce through wet rubber. It was even more relieving to find the sickening rubbing sound ease with each balloon that was popped.

I breezed through the first level and was coasting to victory, but then I got too cocky for my own good and a green spear completely missed its intended target and collided with an unsuspecting purple balloon. The impact was awkward and unnatural. It made an awful screech and the spear was flung backwards towards me. Remarkably, the balloon failed to pop but it now looked significantly weakened and prune like. All the other balloons above it looked destabilised as a result, which seemed strange because some just sat stubbornly in the air from where their neighbours had previously been shot down. This reminded me that I was still in a game and from experience an unforgiving one at that.

The consequence of running out of spears, was something I dared not think about. The happy go lucky character would either get violently swept away by a deluge of burst water balloons or would collapse dramatically on the ground in fatigue if most of the balloons had already been popped. I could not let this happen to me!

Desperate not to make any more errors with the potential for tragedy, I tried to regain my focus. I took my time and sure enough bright blue, artificial sky blossomed from above where the final layer of balloons had been penetrated; with it offering an opportunity to win.

I soon only had five balloons left, all the same deep purple. Annoyingly, each were spaced out horizontally so five spears were needed to do the job. My bag of spears told me I now had seven weapons left to win the battle. I was in a good position but suddenly felt a crippling apprehension at the thought of making another simple error.

The last thing I felt at that point was confident, but I unleashed the last few spears and prayed. Thankfully each one hit; although the final one made me sweat a little as it scraped the left edge, rather than going straight through the middle of the balloon.

As the last gush of water drained away, a multitude of multicoloured firework blasts filled the sky from all directions and a surge of relief, pride and anticipation for what was next filled me with excitement.

Everything melted away from the screen and the miniature jungle island appeared in the distance again. Weirdly the dull balloon was still just that, hollow, but surely not, I had finished the level? However, the stepping-stones were alight, inviting me to proceed, so I must have been successful. A frantic search in all directions for clues soon confirmed my victory; behind me the empty outline of the balloon was gleaming with bright yellow, shining down on me like the sun. It beamed down joyfully on the vast clump of trees that I had seemingly now bypassed.

I gained great pride from my achievement. This was so much better than playing on my pathetic little screen. I was actually involved in the action, and eager to play some more. Drunk with success I walked confidently on to the next level.

As expected, level two looked identical to my first battle. However, this time I knew the creators would up the stakes slightly.

I applied myself in a calm, concentrated and effective way and sure enough it didn't take long for me to unlock the heavens of success above and I smashed through the final balloon to secure victory.

The next level was waiting for my grand entrance. It would be rude not to keep going after my initial success. It unfolded in very much the same way and I was soon in the zone. Several more levels followed, and I soon found the peculiarity of my circumstances melt away and with this I gathered momentum.

Before long the jungle themed levels had run their course and I played my way through circus set ups, which featured oversized and brightly coloured tents along with creepy clown holograms, before moving on to more sinister surroundings.

I eventually reached a level with dark crooked castles which were home to vicious looking bats. The addition of a howling wind that battered wooden windows and a pounding rain, fork lightning and thunder, all added to an off-putting and difficult environment. This was topped off by the continuous playing of a Dracula themed tune.

As in previous levels, I knew what must be done, but I wasn't quite sure where this whole experience was heading. I knew the game was seemingly never ending, after currently approaching the late 200's the normal way. The thought filled me with dread, but I figured this was different, some kind of test even, and I would be able to leave when I had proved my worth. Besides, I had this game nailed to a tee back in the real world and I was confident that I was in the driving seat in this very real immersion.

Aside from my phone high scores, it was rare for me to achieve much in life back home. My grades were pretty average, and I was never any good at sports. If only my parents could see me now (even though this challenge was crazy); I would like to hope they could be proud of me for once.

It was during a game in sinister gothic surroundings that my confidence started to crumble. The balloons got smaller and the number of balloons that were coupled with vertical ease, became less prominent. Several times during one game, I shaved the edges of a balloon and even missed twice with my spear.

It took all the concentration I could muster to keep delivering shots of glory, but wicked visions of what would happen should I fail, started to invade my thoughts. On the rare occasion I did fail a level on my phone I recall the sickening consequence of my partner in crime getting savagely washed away by a Tsunami of water from above. The look of horror on my fictitious friend's face was firmly etched in my mind. This could be me if I made the wrong move.

Somehow, I managed to cast these ill thoughts aside and keep focussed on the task in hand. Each carefully aimed shot hit the intended balloon and victory was getting close.

I decided it was time to find a way out of here after this level. I had no idea how to leave in the middle of a game. If I wanted to leave in real life, I would just close the app, but this wilderness didn't seem to offer such an easy solution. The game had to go on.

The spears kept hitting their targets and I was well over half-way at this point. However just as I started to sense the end was near, my trusty spear collided with a shiny ball loaded with razor sharp spikes. The spear made a sickening clang that echoed in the air before crashing down mere inches in front of me. The spike vibrated but mercifully stayed put for now.

How could I have forgot? After flying through the easy stages, this game liked to throw a few curve balls. Or spike balls in this case. This made things harder, a lot harder. I tried to keep calm. All I had to do was make it through this level and I had the chance to break free.

If my memory served me correctly, and I'm sure it did, these nasty little spikes were hidden randomly amongst the balloons, each one cunningly disguised as the soft rubber pest I aimed to destroy. This grave arrangement knocked me for six as things had now turned into a game of luck. I'm pretty sure there was a strategic route required to avoid catastrophe, but I had never figured it out. I just used to wing it and hope for the best.

Losing the level was never such a big deal when I could simply toss my phone aside in defeat. I had no idea what defeat would mean in this strange new place. Matters were made worse when I suddenly felt a subtle but very human element torture me as I approached halfway through the level. My spear throwing arm started to ache. At first it was just a mild sensation of discomfort but with each spear that was unleashed, the pain intensified. Was this pain all in my head? I wasn't sure, but it sure damn felt real!

I soon began to develop a burn in my shoulder and my arm felt like a steel bar under the strain. Bizarrely my hand action failed to be compromised as a result of my suffering. In fact, I was operating in some kind of autopilot, and I couldn't stop. My brain soon began sending me signals to take a break, but my pixelated body and game brain continued like clockwork.

If this was real life I would likely be sweating with fear. Determined not to get spooked, I took a few moments to compose myself and regain my focus. Just make it to the end of this level I reassured myself. The intense concentration and opportunity of an end of level escape, spurred me to soldier on and I somehow completed the level.

I was again transported to a miniature island which led on to deeper and darker endeavours. There must be a way out by now I thought. My eyes inspected every area of the screen like an alarm sensor. I noticed an abundance of icons scattered above and below me. I couldn't believe I hadn't noticed these earlier. Although they looked to be seemingly weightless, I was now starting to learn that whole experience was littered with illusions.

A random plus symbol appeared in the corner of the screen at the demand of my outstretched arm. I wasn't entirely sure, but I think this button invited more options for me to choose from. I was right. It immediately enlarged after I went in for the click and an options menu appeared on screen. I scanned across the pink blocks, but none offered me an exit option. This made me feel uneasy. The other options included a coin symbol and lightning bolt. I was certain these would offer zero help.

Starting to panic I returned to the previous screen and frantically tried the available options anyway. As expected, they didn't work. Just think you idiot, I shouted at myself with sheer determination. This did the trick. God, I had been so stupid. Why had I not thought of this from the beginning?

I thrust my hand straight down below me, reaching down as far as I could. Miraculously a big white rectangular button laced with Chrome appeared as if by magic. I pressed it hard and was transported back to the home screen in an instant.

8

EXPLORATION

Relief hit me like a strong shot of coffee! I was suddenly giddy at my success. The fear that had begun to boil up inside me, was now starting to simmer down. As I stood staring back at the home screen, any urgency to leave I may have had, was now evaporating. Instead I stood and considered my options for some time. Now feeling energised at realising I hadn't been harmed during my game play, I couldn't wait to immerse myself in another adventure. I could do just about anything I wanted in here. The idea of being inside a video or spy on my friend's social media on a grand scale, was a thrill to think about.

All the apps I knew so well were glowing invitingly, just for me. I just couldn't decide where to explore first. On the third row of apps I was drawn towards a bright orange head with three speech bubbles escaping his mouth. This was labelled Socialise and was basically just another of the many messaging apps that could be used. Great for private chats, but not exactly the most exciting one to discover, given the power I'd been granted.

Straight ahead of me resided a big goofy looking emoji head with a beaming smile and wild dreadlocks that sprouted like rainbows from her crown. I couldn't help but mirror her joyful expression as I thought about what fun this app would bring. The app was called Emojime and this seemed more like the place for an adventure. I therefore wasted no time in embracing the wonders I knew it would have in store. My pressing directive instantly transported me to the action once more.

It was no real shock to see the app's fool-proof menu appear before me. After all I used it every day. It was freaky to see it on such a large scale though; the bright yellow navigational words simply hovering in mid-air, surrounded by an endless amount of orange.

I was gifted with three options to choose from; Chat, Map and Personalise.

Given that Chat was my go-to way of gossiping with friends, it seemed like a good place to explore first. At this point it first occurred to me that I wasn't actually cut off from the world in my current crazy state. I was in my phone and therefore had every connection to the outside world I could ever need; and this undeniable connection couldn't have been closer to home as my family group chat conversation was in my immediate eye-line. In an instant I was reminded of my earlier rage towards the parents and it threatened again to burst my bubble. I still felt so hurt by their wicked actions, that I was in no mood to forgive them. Well not anytime soon, that's for sure.

I considered for a second how random it would be to chat with anyone about my current situation. What would I say, 'Hey mum I won't be going out tonight as I'm just playing inside my phone?' The insanity of the thought made me chuckle for a moment. No one appeared online anyway and in fact none of my close friends were either, so I decided to move on to something else. It wasn't that unusual for no one to be online. Most people used other apps to chat these days, but for some reason this confirmation still made me feel uneasy.

Time to explore the map. The thought of this was exciting, as this was no ordinary sketch of the world. After pressing the bottom left corner button, to return to the home screen, I began to surf the virtual sea of discovery. In contrast to my phone map, this was quite simply spectacular. I found myself engulfed in a vast computerised, imaginary world. Your average Joe, using an ordinary phone would just see this map in a basic birds-eye view, but my view right now was something else. I remained my new virtual self, but remarkably found that I was in a fictional recreation of my bedroom, but without walls. This enabled me to see miles of 3D land outside my house. Rather than fully fledged houses surrounding me, there was just flat outlines of their bases.

Although this initially seemed odd, I soon realised this was done intentionally by the app creators. Dotted amongst the mass of stump buildings and fake greenery, were the oversized figures of my animated friends. Even though their locations were scattered throughout town and beyond, everyone was in clear view. It was wonderful to see the likes of Sammy, Megan and even precious Jade, just standing and smiling intently in wait.

The whole set up was so comical it made me laugh again. Except I couldn't laugh, not in the normal sense of the word anyway. Instead, a winding reel of purple bubbled 'Ha Ha' text spurted uncontrollably from my beaming mouth and vanished in mid-air several feet about my head. This crazy occurrence just made me laugh more which unleashed even more comic style text. It escaped from me like rapid fire. In that moment, all the anger and worries from the past few days simply washed away.

After a good while the giddiness subsided and so I decided to leave the confines of the house to embrace the wonders of this new world.

I found I could move quite freely in any direction that I desired. I walked straight through the imaginary walls of my house and in the direction of my nearest emoji friend. I walked across the stumps of neighbour's houses but couldn't see any of the inner buildings unfortunately. What a nosy bitch I was, but it would have been cool to see. I walked over gardens, straight through trees, in the middle of roads and through alley ways.

Just like in any normal phone map, there was no live people or moving cars. So, I basically had the freedom to go or do whatever I wanted.

In no time at all, I approached the local park and noticed a big splodge of blue where the lake would usually be. Just to confirm that I could walk anywhere, I decided to cross it. Clearly still not 100% in this theory I found myself approach it at a run. This action not only allowed me to cross the lake unscathed, it actually propelled me across in an instant. I moved at lightning speed.

This certainly made up for those grim sports days having to endure the pain of finishing last. I continued to run and before I knew it, the park was well out of sight. Reminding myself that this was a map, it suddenly made sense that my action of running was like zooming in on a place you wanted to go.

I ran straight toward my friend Lucy who lived just a few streets behind the park. When I say we were friends, we weren't actually proper friends. In fact, we hadn't spoken in years. We used to be inseparable back in primary school, but then it all went down the pan in year 7 when 'Miss Loved by Everyone' Jade swooped in. Since then it was rare for me to get a 'hi'.

Nonetheless, it was absolutely mind-blowing to see her as a life-size emoji. She was swaying slightly in what I would imagine was her bedroom. Her hair was a deep ruby red and Lucy had clearly put emphasis on her matching colour lip pout and boob size. She also radiated a slight digitalised glow which was just another reminder that it was all made-up.

I had little time to dwell on how unbelievable this all appeared before Lucy's emoji sprung to life. She had suddenly changed into baby pink pyjama shorts with a white strappy top and now seemed to be sitting like a genie with her legs crossed. What's more, Lucy looked like she was whistling, but instead of noise, bright blue music notes floated elegantly out of her mouth. Meanwhile her hands held a gold pair of straighteners which rhythmically motored through her hair.

Of course, people could update their emoji to mimic what they were doing. Mine was very often set to smashing an oversized gaming joypad or curled up on an imaginary pillow, unleashing huge zzz's.

Again, seeing this feature in life-sized glory was truly hilarious, but then it occurred to me that Lucy was quite obviously getting ready for Jade's stupid party and this put a massive dampener on my bubbly mood. I decided to move on.

There were several friends in the near vicinity, and I couldn't decide which one to head towards. All I knew is that Lucy had angered me, and I was determined to swat away any more ill feelings about the party.

As I wondered aimlessly on, it occurred to me that I was close to Brad's house. His emoji was in fact smiling directly ahead of me. Just like our time in detention I found myself drawn like a magnet towards him. A rush of excitement enveloped me, even at the thought of seeing him in digital form. I was about to get up close and personal. Well, kind of. I often daydreamed about actually getting this intimate. Perhaps when all this was over, I might get my chance to do just that. But for now, virtual stalking would have to do.

All anger towards Lucy had gone. It was replaced with longing and excitement instead. I was in a frenzy to witness whatever awesome actions Brad's made-up self was occupied with. In fact, I broke into a run again in order to find out and reached him in pretty much an instant.

Omg, even as an emoji he looked fit. His jet-black hair was perfectly ruffled, and he wore thick sunshades and a lovely khaki T-shirt. I mean, he had clearly given his other self much bigger muscles than the real Brad, but it just added to my fantasies.

Unlike Lucy's emoji, he was already occupied. In fact, he was buzzing with energy. His emoji was aggressively strumming a beasty-looking electric guitar. His hand moved so violently across the strings, it was just a blur. At the same time his head rocked back and forth whilst his oversized boots tapped along to whatever tune he was playing.

Every strum bought with it, fake, silver music notes that escaped from the guitar, along with bright yellow forks of lighting. What a sight it was.

I just stood and watched for…I don't even know how long. I just admired his perfect smile and big blue eyes. It was a shame I couldn't actually hear the music he was playing. I could have stayed there all day.

He seemed so engrossed in the music that it filled me with hope. Perhaps Brad wasn't bothering with Jade's party? Perhaps he had decided to give it a miss as he clearly had better things to do than spend time with that bitch? As soon as this joyful thought crossed my mind however, Brad's guitar simply vanished; and then moments later, so did Brad.

I turned around to see his emoji was drifting away from his street, as though on a travellator. He was no longer alone, as the figure of a lad with flaming orange hair walked in sync away from the house beside him. I knew the figure was that of Brad's annoying best friend Jake. It was obvious where they were going, and it filled me with grief. I turned away from them both as I didn't need confirmation of what I already knew. Instead I turned back and headed home.

As I had already figured, it could have taken me mere moments to return home, but instead I meandered woefully slowly through the digitalised streets, questioning what had become of my life. Oversized, sky-blue drops began to cascade out of nowhere beside where I walked. It was clear that they were falling from my eyes. My emoji was crying. The tears seemed to go on and on, creating fake puddles at my feet.

I diverted from the pit of self-pity because, without even meaning to, I approached Sammy's house. This immediately ignited thoughts of me abandoning our plans for the night and, to make matters worse, her emoji looked a bit sad too. She sported a blank expression, holding a T.V. remote and a brightly coloured ice-cream tub. I should have felt bad, guilty even, but all I could think about was my own torment at having to endure the fact that everyone was about to enjoy a killer party.

Unlike the other emoji friends, I didn't stop at Sammy's for entertainment. Instead, I pressed on back to my imaginary house. Just then, a thought occurred to me; what would I actually do when I returned home?

I was ready to delve into what other delights my phone might have in store, preferably some that did not remind me of that wretched party. I still had the personalise function to tackle yet, but I didn't feel in the mood to mess around with the way my emoji looked at that moment. I don't think a change of clothes or hair colour would deter Brad from going the party, so there was absolutely no point. When I couldn't immediately see a way out of the map from where I stood, I figured the answer must be at home.

A short time later I arrived back. It was like returning to a bird nest, filling me with a sense of warmth and safety. Upon entering my room, this sense of security was soon shattered with shock however, as an unfamiliar emoji magically pinged beside me.

The mysterious figure was one of teenage girl - no doubt a similar age to me. She stood there, smiling as if we were the best of friends; but even amongst the few friends I had whose emojis looked nothing like them, I was certain I did not recognise this one. She had bright blonde hair held back in a ponytail, big green eyes and she wore super-baggy, blue dungarees with chunky flip-flops. Even by current standards (where anything goes in fashion), the dress sense seemed a little odd to me. I'm pretty sure none of my friends wore anything like that.

I was so stunned, I just stood there for a few moments, glaring at the girl. Then she spoke. Not in animated text talk this time like my emoji friends, but in actual human like, real-life noise.

'Hi Lindsey, I've been expecting you,' she said enthusiastically, in a friendly if not slightly automated voice.

Words still escaped me as the shock of this comment continued to make waves. How did she know my name? Why would she be expecting me?

'Hi,' I found myself replying. 'Who are you ... and how do you know my name?'

Smiling at my response, she replied with yet more enthusiasm. 'I'm here to help you. My name is Jemma and I'm here to have a chat about how you use your phone.'

I'm not sure what response I was expecting, but it definitely wasn't that. This weirdo didn't even answer my question. Well she did, I guess... kind of. It didn't even matter, it sounded as though she was here to help, that was the main thing. The thought at being shown how to fully immerse myself into all the many wonders of this new land definitely piqued my interest. Perhaps Jemma was a more advanced and definitely creepier version of those virtual assistant things.

'Ok. That's great. Do you know how I can get back to the home page?' I enquired.

Returning my question with another automated-looking smile, Jemma responded, 'Yes of course, but I think you already know the answer Lindsey.'

What the hell, I thought. Was this some kind of test? I felt like saying, 'why not just tell me?' but then thought I best not be rude. I had no idea who this person/robot girl was, and I did not want to annoy her/it.

'Ok, let me think,' I said.

Jemma didn't respond but just acknowledged my participation in her little game with a nod.

I racked my brains for a few minutes, trying not to get distracted by Jemma who made me feel a bit uneasy as she stood there, just watching me.

When I actually decided to use my brain, the answer was really simple. I just had to replicate what I did last time; reach down for the home button again. Controlling my own fate in here really wasn't that hard.

'Ok, I think I know how to go back,' was the response I offered Jemma. 'I'm guessing I just need to reach down for the home button, which I did to leave the Balloon Trouble app?'

Jemma looked at me with glee. It was a bit OTT to be honest.

'Great work Lindsey. I'm sure you will agree the answer was actually really simple when you think about it.'

Ok, Miss Smart-Ass, no need to patronise me. She was right though, I guess.

'Well, that's good to know. Yes, it was actually,' I reluctantly admitted. 'But what do you think I should do when I get back to the home page?' I then enquired.

For some reason, my question seemed to drain Jemma's enthusiasm. Her creepy grin was replaced by a blank expression.

'That's totally your choice Lindsey, but my question to you would be, is that really the question you need to be asking me?'

Ok this girl was starting to weird me out a bit now. What on earth did she mean by that? I wanted to fire some sassy comments her way and I probably would have done if I wasn't terrified of what she might do. Jemma said she was here to help me, so I decided to continue playing her annoying game.

'Ok, but I don't know what question I need to ask. Are you able to tell me?' I asked.

Jemma's blank look now seemed to radiate disappointment.

'I'm afraid if you do not know the question, then you are not yet ready, Lindsey,' she replied.

Ok I was done with this freakish thing. This just seemed like a game and I wasn't in the mood to play right now. I was not convinced she could really help. I would figure out what to do on my own. 'I see. Well it's ok, I will be leaving now and will give it some thought,' I replied, trying not to sound too sarcastic.

'Thanks for helping me figure the way out,' I added.

Jemma's expression remained unmoved as I prepared to leave. Just as I reached down for the home button, however, she spoke to me once more.

'Bye for now, Lindsey. I wish you luck. Just try to remember what's true. And don't forget ... you have the power.'

Again, I had no idea what she was on about. I responded with thanks and thrust my hand deep down into the imaginary ground until the big white button appeared like an obedient dog and transported me back to the home page.

9

FOOD FOR THOUGHT

Thankfully, my actions had worked. Jemma and the Emojime app had disappeared. I was faced with the familiar home screen and it made me feel slightly more secure.

As much as I was excited for another adventure, I couldn't shake off thoughts about the advice (I guess you could call it) that Jemma had just handed out to me. I still had no idea what she was on about, but it did not sound positive, and that made me feel uneasy.

Determined to block out her voice that chorused in my mind, I decided to plunge straight into another fantasy.

The first app in the bottom corner of my screen had a big, blue play symbol that was labelled videos. Wow being inside a video would be incredible. Surely 3D, 4D or even VR would have nothing on what I could experience here.

I didn't hesitate to reach out and was whisked away to another new world. Big, bold blocks of imagery and a giant search bar then consumed my curious face. I was now a player in this unusual game, and I didn't need any instruction to attack the search bar.

It quickly became obvious I didn't need a pen to write. I knew I had the power; and so I began to swoosh my hand to form exciting letters. It didn't even take me long to decide on a search. I had longed to watch my favourite artist in concert last year. Some of the other girls went to watch him in London, but it was no surprise that I was prohibited. I was gutted. The pain of missing out was all but forgotten in this moment though as my hand etched perfectly formed block letters that formed the words 'Rohnan Blues Live at the O2 2014'. I felt drunk with power, elated even. This experience was magic.

Again, everything dissolved around me. The hairs on the back of my neck became as straight as arrows as I was plunged into the heart of the action.

The atmosphere was electric. Over 20,000 people packed out the arena. A large rectangular stage lay at the centre of the place, and from it protruded another stage, this time long and narrow that created a walkway through the mass of rowdy fans.

Straight ahead of me, strobe lights penetrated my eyes and large electronic screens that emitted colourful imagery of butterflies wearing leather jackets and coiled snakes that sported shiny gold rings, sat snugly around their smooth bodies, were propped up at either side of the stage. The sound of Rohnan's rustic voice echoed around the arena and so did the thousands of voices that embraced the lyrics.

Rohnan was perched on what looked like a modest wooden stool, looking immensely cool in ripped jeans, his blond hair wrenched back into a top knot. He strummed intently on an acoustic guitar, his eyes closed as he offered his voice to the crowd, only opening them to acknowledge the crowd's feedback, which was wild.

In a transfixed state, I had failed to notice my peculiar perspective of the show. I was perched precariously above the crowd. I looked like a wondrous genie, floating above the rest and asserting my power. Moreover, I was invisible to the revellers below, as a loud scream of excitement from myself confirmed.

As I delved more deeply into my surroundings, it soon became clear that I wasn't quite the almighty. As I tried to explore 360 degrees, an invisible block crippled my ability to see any further than a 180-degree angle. Furthermore, my whole body was continually being manoeuvred (sometimes violently) in a wealth of directions, dependant on Rohnan's stage presence and tone of song. I felt like a rag doll being toyed with, and it soon made me feel disorientated.

I had no idea how long the video was on for. I wish I had checked. As Rohnan moved on to his livelier numbers, the crowd got more excited and I got thrust around even more. Being able to pass out at that moment would have been a blessing. But I didn't. How could I - I wasn't even real?

Just as I began a plea for the video to stop, my wish was granted. A series of violent vibrations screamed like a naughty toddler through the screen and instantly brought everything to a halt. Two huge, blue message blocks invaded the screen above my head and stubbornly sat there waiting for me to deal with them. All the while everything from Rohnan's gig was frozen in action. Everything except me.

My heart sank as the first message was from my dad. The message only allowed me to read a couple of lines, but it was enough to puncture me with guilt.

'I just thought you should know that your mum is really upset that you would rather spend the night glued to that phone ...'

As if that wasn't bad enough, I could tell that the message directly above was from Sammy. I purposely avoided its judgemental stare. I knew it would be packed with anger after (deliberately or not) trashing our plans.

Thankfully, the messages didn't show for very long and everything sprung back to life, throwing me back into the mosh pit.

Eventually Rohnan moved on to some more chilled out acoustic music and the movements became more of a light sway. It was enough for me to regain my thoughts and realise that I was moving in sync with someone's phone. Someone was filming, and not very well for that matter.

Aside from the realisation of what was going on, this also gave me time to dwell on the dreaded messages that had just hijacked me. These coupled with the worrying words of that weird Jemma girl, suddenly made me think it might now be a good time to figure out how to get the hell out of here.

As much as this experience was spectacular, an uneasiness about the whole thing started to settle and grow like a thorn bush within me. As the motion sickness finally began to subside though, the soft, sweet voice of Rohnan made me drift away for a second and momentarily push this fear aside.

I looked into the crowd and could see the section where my friends would have been at this very moment, loving life; with that everything went black again before I was thrust back to the video's search screen.

Relief flooded me upon return to what was relative normality, or rather eccentric calm. However, I soon started to experience mental fatigue as I gazed at the multitude of vibrant colours that canvassed the entire space in front of me. Now I had watched one more cheeky video here, it really was best to conjure up some ideas on how to get back to the perfectly dull reality; that is, home and my normal life.

I looked again at the screen and created an upright movement which allowed me to scroll down the page. An array of thumbnail images whizzed wildly across the screen, many of which craved my attention. I resisted the temptation to click on one.

I scrolled and scrolled, but seemingly endless amounts of videos offered me the opportunity to view. Acting like an over absorbed sponge, I couldn't stop my brain from consuming every visual in sight. I tried scrolling faster in search of the bottom, but this merely accelerated a seemingly infinite reel.

It also soon became clear that these thumbnails all represented videos I had previously searched for or watched. Everything from surfing swans to rapper goes crazy at camera man; it was fascinating yet disturbing to see.

The scrolling went on and on without any sign of stopping. I could tell my brain had turned to mush again. It was as though the phone's actions had taken over.

I gave my head a shake, closed my eyes and managed to stop scrolling. I stood with my eyes closed for what seemed like a lifetime, straining to figure out how to get off the video page. My thoughts felt like a blunt axe swinging at a dense tree as they remained fixated on the magic of the gig I had just watched.

Eventually I knew I had to focus on the task at hand and like a bolt from above, the recurring answer struck me again. I simply had to reach down for the chrome home screen button. My thought was immediately axed by a counter thought that this couldn't possibly work again. It was just far too simple. None the less I reached down with hope and once again the button answered my exit call, appearing to whisk me back to the home page.

I don't know why I'd been over-thinking things. The get out of jail card was the same each time and yet I was too distracted each time to use basic common sense. This was my phone; and I knew exactly how to use it! I just needed to stop being an idiot if I wanted to leave the sneaky game.

After realising this, I spent some time just to think; and in fact, it really didn't take me long to figure out that I needed to actively turn off the phone to leave for good. I needed to blacken the screen or turn the phone off all together. I swelled with pride at my theory and used the moment of enthusiasm to figure out how best to shut the thing down.

The first and most obvious thought was to manually turn the phone off, but as I gazed ahead at the bright and beautiful colours straight ahead of me, poisonous thoughts started to creep back in my brain. A shut down would surely plunge me into darkness. What if my theory was wrong? What if my actions locked me into the phone forever? What if I became a permanent emoji and could only ever live within these four curved edges? Worst still, what if turning out the light on my phone, turned out my own light? The thought was enough to cripple me with terror.

Right stay calm Lindsey, think positive.

The dreaded thought of eternal darkness haunted me, but it occurred to me that I was thinking of the worst-case scenario. What's more, it seemed even less likely that this would be my fate if I hit the reset button instead. At least if I did this, I was likely to come back again, even if it wasn't to reality.

My thoughts were suddenly blessed with images of rebirth and the opportunity to make a fresh start. It soon became quite clear that this resolution actually offered little in the way of hope as there was no way that I could actually reach the reset button. The reset button was in fact the long and slim slither that controlled the phone's volume, but it also acted as a reset if held down for a couple of seconds. Even though the button was large and looked within my reach, I was far from confident about being able to provide enough sustained pressure to reset, but I had to at least give it a go.

As I walked across the colourless ground below, I started to worry about the thought of accidentally ramping up the volume if something went wrong in my reset attempt, which could make my experience much more lethal. I quickly snapped out of it, however, when an imaginary force halted my advance to a standstill at what was presumably the edge of the phone screen. I should have expected this after my failure to reach my Thailand wallpaper earlier. I primed myself for action. After stretching out my hand, I jumped up high, but with cruel predictability confirmed that the button was out of reach by mere inches, even after I took God knows how many energetic leaps of faith.

It was at this point it occurred to me that I hadn't even tried to turn around to look what lay behind me. I was so consumed about the wonders that the enlarged phone phenomenon offered in front of my very eyes, that I hadn't given this a shred of thought. The realisation made my blood chill. I had no idea what I would find. If I was in fact inside my own smartphone, perhaps I was able to look at what it looks like to be looking out of the phone; into a mammoth sized version of my bedroom perhaps? Maybe my furniture would look like colossal skyscrapers. Does that mean that I had been shrunk? It was a troubling thought; one of many at that moment. If I recall the giant loading bar from earlier, it was quite clearly growing wildly out of control and this made me fairly confident that it was the phone that had miraculously grown and not me who had been squashed. Given the craziness of the evening though, I wasn't ruling anything out.

There was only one way to find out and with great

trepidation I started to make a 180-degree turn.

The result wasn't quite what I had expected. I was faced with a great sheet of translucent glass, speckled with little scuffs here and there. Remarkably I couldn't see anything through the glass. Instead I seemed to be incarcerated by a blurry grey wall of material. It reminded me a bit like frosted glass that people have in their bathroom windows, to ensure privacy. Clearly whoever or whatever decided to cage me in here, did not wish for anyone to accidentally intrude. I reached out my hand but there was nothing to touch. I tried to walk towards the ominous substance, but an invisible force prevented it.

I looked up and down several times and at first could see a white top and bottom. Then I noticed a big black crack that etched itself across the white and grey like giant spindly spider's legs. Oh yes, this was definitely the glass on my phone. I would recognise that crack anywhere. It pissed me off every day that I was such an idiot to break it so soon, and there was nothing I could do about it. All for a stupid bathroom selfie, that probably looked grim as I didn't even get a pic back from Brad anyway. I couldn't afford to fix it and my parents refused to, simply to teach me a lesson. Thoughts of their unfairness again filled me with anger.

I refused to let panic muscle in at this expected failure and the confirmation that there was in fact no immediate way out. I further reassured myself that this whole trippy experience could in fact be a dream after all and no matter what I did it would soon be over when I woke up. It all seemed so real that I wasn't convinced at this wishful thought, but another look at the serene screen ahead offered me hope.

After all, the out of body experiences that potentially lay ahead in my quest to leave, was still an exciting prospect. For some bizarre reason I developed a powerful urge to explore again. A voice in my head convinced me that my key to leave lay hidden deep within the phone and it was my destiny to find out what it was.

Thoughts flitted through my mind about what to do next and I soon came up with a wild yet ingenious theory that I had to work my way across and up the screen until I reached the reset button. It was definitely worth a shot.

Maybe if I worked my way diagonally or up across the apps, this would act like stepping stones where I could leap frog across each app, eventually reaching the final one which would clear a path to the reset button? From here I would just reconfigure the phone and return myself to my normal state? My plan sounded simple enough to follow even if I wasn't fully convinced that this theory would work; but I had to try something.

I walked back as far I was able, to the bottom left hand of my screen and was powerfully drawn back towards the ocean blue videos button. This would be the first stepping-stone to take, but it quickly occurred to me that I had already been there and got the T-shirt with this app having already explored videos a short while ago.

I figured out my next step towards freedom would be to relive the Balloon Trouble game again. True I could happily play the game all day, but the thought of retracing my steps was now starting to sound a bit ridiculous. After all I had not been relocated to a higher level where the app was homed. I had been transported back to the bottom of the phone once more and this meant the next app was no closer and I was no closer to the exit. Clearly my theory must be wrong, and this was a worry.

Back to the drawing board.

Surely, I could reach the reset button, it would just take some more willpower. Maybe I would have to just swerve my involvement in the phone adventure after all? This would be a shame, but the sensible side of me knew that getting out of here was critical. After all, the top of screen was only a couple of feet higher than me. Although I couldn't actually see the reset button, this had to mean that it was only a short reach from it. I just had to jump a little higher and walk as close to the edge as possible.

Here goes nothing.

I leapt like a dolphin leaving water with my arm fully extended, but I was miles away. I tried again and again and even attempted to twist my arm to the right as I peaked. Eventually after an anger fuelled attempt, I could feel an imaginary curve and the solid cold of my phone's chrome finish. A wave of excitement hit me like a truck. It definitely felt like a physical sensation for the first time in ages.

Inspired by the sensation, I decided to jump again. This time I threw everything I could muster into it. Remarkably I felt a bump in the road again. I couldn't believe it. It was definitely a button; and in mid-flight, I pressed it. I immediately wished I hadn't. My whole body was suddenly shrunk by several feet.

It looked as though my joy ride so far was ending in a crash. Fear now clamped down on me like a vice. It felt as I had just swallowed a rock. I wanted to panic, but then my mind caught up with the fact I had no human functions and so it did nothing for me. As soon as this became clear I tumbled on to the denseless floor below which I'm sure wouldn't have taken the weight of the normal human being I wish that I was. It was in this moment that I could have cried, but in this world even tears weren't around to make you feel better; not real ones anyway.

10

COMMUNICATION

Shortly after starting to bask in a pit of self-pity, I was startled by a short ping that sent visible shock waves across the screen and made me vibrate for a moment. It was the weirdest sensation. I wasn't immediately sure what had caused this strange phenomenon. As I looked across the screen, I realised that the little orange social media head symbol that poured out 3 lines of speech (which was frustratingly only two steps away from my escape), had a bright red little three symbol floating above it.

Of course, I had received some notifications. This exciting new revelation reminded me again that I was in fact in a phone and therefore had every connection to the outside world I could have hoped for. At this, my enthusiasm re-joined the party. All I had to do was cry out for help.

Drunk on hope, I immediately reached for the reassuring, yellow envelope text message icon (that was bang in front of me) and started to debate on who to ask for help. However, my voice of reason again muscled in to smother my ambitions. What the hell would I say? Who would believe me? How could they even help me?

The small ray of hope I had created quickly extinguished and it became clear that ending this crazy ride was going to be no piece of cake. What's more the thoughts of addressing the dreaded texts from earlier, again entered my mind.

I pressed the text message icon anyway and a vast list of contacts and their recent one line of message appeared before my eyes. Before I had too much time to formulate a prison break, I was almost wounded with more ill fortune when I realised I had several more messages from Sammy. Annoyingly they were taunting me at the top of the screen, well out of arms reach. I felt helpless. It then occurred to me that I had an additional shortcut bar at the bottom of the screen for frequently used contacts.

The shortcut appeared in a circular shape which emitted the letter S. As soon as I touched the shortcut, our endless stream of conversation boxes appeared. Sammy's most recent message radiated at the bottom of the screen like a gift cast down from the gods. A mere glance at the message strangled this feeling of euphoria though as it simply reminded me of my wicked ways.

Even in my miniaturised state, I could easily read the words of Sammy's first message which had taken a back seat on the conversation stream position; in fact, the words looked gigantic still and were equally as wounding.

'Hey you get my last txt? What time did you have in mind? I'm not doing anything so just come round wen you ready. Convinced ma mum to let us have a cheeky bottle of wine ☺ lol What you fancy doin for food? I reckon we order pizza xxx.'

I allowed the words to pierce me several times, determined that they would sound less thoughtful with each read; but they didn't. Why did I have to be so stubborn? Why did I have to be so sour about not being allowed to go to Jade's pathetic party?

The second message read, 'Hey you there…? But guessing you did an still getting ready ha ha just let us know wen you heading out ☺ xxx.'

The innocent nature of the message cut through me like a knife. After all, I could have been there with my best friend, right now. We would already be about to open a bottle of wine and I can only dream of how good that cheesy pizza would taste.

I had little time to dwell on the content however, as just at that moment another bright blue message box popped up in front of my face. I immediately knew I didn't want to read it.

After a few moments of cowardly eye closing, I bit the bullet and read the text. 'Hey, guessing you decided not to bother tonight then. You somehow manage to sneak an invite to the party after all? Ha ha a tb would have been nice like but oh well ☺ x.'

The killer blow confirmed that I had been stuck in this prison for several hours, at least. How on earth had so much time passed? I was a lamb that had just been sent for slaughter. Imaginary tears didn't flow down my face, but real ones flooded my thorny heart.

At that point, something just jolted in my brain like it had been prodded with a white-hot poker. I frantically started to type a reply to justify and defend my actions. Fortunately, I was dramatically laboured in my eagerness to do something I might regret by the difficult actions involved in typing on an imaginary keyboard that was ten times the usual size. It was like playing an intense game of 'whack-a-mole'.

'Believe me, I wanted to come round but the weirdest thing has happened to me. I know it sounds crazy but I've been shrunk and sucked into my phone. I know it sounds unbelievable but you've gotta believe me. I'm really freaking out.' I restrained myself from typing out anything else, realising the rambling I had just plastered all over the screen ahead sounded absurd. I wiped away the message. Who in their sane mind would believe such a crazy story? I managed to compose myself and decided it best to delete the text. Time to think, Lindsey!

11

THE PARTY

Feeling like a caged animal at this point, I started to despair. I had every connection to the outside world in my fingertips, but no way of breaking through the barrier. Worse still, the message situation reminded me that I had no idea what the actual time was, only that a good few hours must have passed. I looked up to the top right of the phone screen but couldn't work out what the digits were in my miniaturised state. Gosh, was my eyesight really that bad?

Perhaps I was just being paranoid at this point, but the time looked suspiciously blurry to me. It was as though I shouldn't have had a problem making out the digits on screen, but I did. It was also a bit suspicious that the texts were not time and dated. I could have sworn they were usually. The more I strained to see the time, the blurrier it appeared. Anyway, the recent message at least half-confirmed that it must still be the 21st, but who knows for sure? Something fishy was clearly going on here and I didn't like it one bit.

This was even more frustrating when all the apps in my immediate view now looked enormous, their vibrant colours an assault on my beady eyes. It was like being in the immediate eyeline of a giant electronic billboard in a city centre.

I just stood there thinking until my head hurt felt mashed. There was just no possible way that I could call for an escape plan. I had no idea how long I had been here for. The situation was starting to seem very scary.

It wasn't too long until I pined for my mum to come and save me. I considered calling her. The urge was so strong. I just didn't care anymore. It didn't matter if the whole world thought I was crazy, my mum would always be there for me if I needed her help.

I even navigated myself towards the dial button as the thought consumed me. I would just go on a wild rant, throw all my cards on the table and let her take over. She was sure to have a solution.

My hand leaned to dial, but then a ping that went off like a loaded cannon made me instinctively retreat. I couldn't believe my eyes. It was another social media notification. Becky is live now. It instantly registered that she would be at the party; it's all she had bragged on about since the invite. Becky was one of Jade's closest cronies and she was always craving attention from wherever she could get it.

I had all but forgot about the wretched party but even though I actively disliked Becky, I hoped (or rather prayed) that this notification would offer an opportunity for escape. Although I had lost faith in being propelled through the apps to a reset button, I figured that anything that could potentially move me around the screen might just offer me some kind of exit solution. I don't know what I expected might happen, but I had no better, or in fact, any, ideas at this point.

I usually felt so sure about everything, but by now I was completely winging it and had no clue what carnage was in store. I had to try something; and so, I pressed the orange block screen, allowing it to drag me back to a warped form of reality once more.

Sure enough, I found myself in Jade's dimly-lit living room. Being in the grasp of a drunken holder, I immediately found myself being tossed around a little bit. At this point, I was getting so determined to leave, I didn't care about the discomfort caused by the phone. My plan to reach the reset was alive once more and hope clung to me like a child clutching its mother.

Hardcore drum and bass music pounded my ears. I could see a lad from the other half of the year hoisting some speakers over his head like it was a World Cup trophy he was showing off, all the while sporting a nonsensical grimace. Some of his mates surrounded him, jumping around like a shrewdness of excited apes.

People were sprawled out on the sofa, some of whom looked to be either passed out or asleep, despite the unrelenting noise. Becky was actively provoking people, slurring her words at people as she thrust her phone into random faces whilst simultaneously video streaming them.

'Put some Rohnan on Connor,' Becky demanded to the spirited self-proclaimed DJ. He seemed oblivious to the request and just continued to bounce along to his tracks. She swiftly moved on to the few people raving in the middle of the dance floor. 'Cut us your shapes then!' which was met with a chorus of cheers.

'Wey I'm stacking shelves!' shouted a giddy girl called Lauren who swayed back and forth as she tried to imitate shelf stacking.

Becky quickly got bored and turned sharply towards the sea of lifeless souls that were in a comatose state on the couch.

'Oi you wasted fuckers, give us a wave?' Becky demanded, at which two skinny lads who looked to be from the year below seemed to give their last efforts at acting crazy, each shouting half-hearted insults at the camera.

Becky quickly got bored again and undertook a grand tour of the house where clusters of energetic people, many of which grasping WKDs or raiding what looked like a parent's booze stash, offered some kind of obscenity at the camera as it soared by.

Becky's commentary got funnier as she went on, and for several minutes I was utterly amused. This allowed me to temporarily forget my unusual view.

'See these lot of absolute piss-heads. I'm not pissed at all you see; I've only had ... how many wines have I had?' slurred Becky at her bestie and my former friend Lucy, who was wearing stupidly-high heels; her bright blonde extensions swaying in and out the frame. Seeing the two girls stumble around like wild animals actually made me quite glad not to be there. Well, not really there anyway.

'Bae, you've only had two wines. You need more!' At which she picked up a half bottle of rosé and attempted to fill up an empty glass she found that had been abandoned on the side.

Becky clearly didn't believe her own revelation and quickly moved on upon realising the drink was for her. She knew she had had way too much already and was starting to feel queasy. It was unlikely her slim frame could handle much more underage abuse.

Becky started to venture upstairs, which seemed to be less rowdy and looked as though it should and probably was, off limits. For some reason, this recent development made me feel uneasy. This wasn't helped by the fact she kept falling on the stairs which made me feel even more disorientated.

There was something about the invasion of privacy I didn't like. There was a sick feeling building in my gut that I was about to become an accomplice to a crime. I didn't like it at all but tried to suppress the thought.

As she reached the top, I could hear someone being violently sick and it made me want to vom. Upon hearing this, Becky broke into hysterics and shouted 'Lightweight' in his direction, at which no response was forthcoming.

She then proceeded to open bedroom doors.

Given that the upstairs was a baron wasteland, with the exclusion of a puking mess, Becky was pushing the boundaries by her navigation off-piste. I started to feel very uncomfortable at this point. I knew Becky was crossing a line and I somehow felt a part of the devious deed. I just reminded myself that I could be a step closer to some sort of exit plan if I could just seize a chance when Becky stopped dragging me round like a ragdoll, or when the live video antics ceased.

The first door she tried was locked. The second was dark and derelict, besides the faint outline of Disney princesses that were plastered on the wall.

'Oops, stay away from the kid's room,' Becky chuckled to herself upon disturbing the innocence that lay within.

The front view video was no longer amusing. I somehow felt equally responsible for this violation of privacy. I started to hope Becky would come to a moral awakening and end the video before she crossed any more lines. But she didn't.

She went for the next door as if on treasure hunt, but what she found was far from gold. My heart stopped at the grave sight that penetrated my eyes. Host Jade lay half naked on top of what was unmistakeably...Brad.

Even though the darkness within was filled with only a faint glimmer of light, the image of Jade's slim, half-naked body and slightly ruffled, black-brunette hair resting on top of Brad's lightly muscled body, was bolted to my brain and it made my stomach do cartwheels.

'Close the fucking door!' Jade screeched in rage at Becky, thrusting a pillow at her; presumably to try and hide what was now in plain sight. At this, she quickly jolted the door back closed and retreated as though she had been hit by a thousand volts. She knew she had crossed the line and suddenly everything disappeared and was replaced by darkness; at last.

12

SCARY DISTRACTIONS

I instantly reappeared facing the giant digital chess board that was the phone home screen, confined to an ocean of nothingness once more. This time the stillness was soothing, the blazing concoction of colour now felt comforting and the failure to escape irrelevant. Anything is better than what I had just endured.

In an attempt to mentally extinguish the pain of seeing Brad and Jade in bed together, I tried to cry but tears failed to flood down my cheeks. Why would they, I'm not even human anymore? I decided to lie on the ocean of nothingness beneath me instead. It seemed like a natural thing to do given my turmoil. Again, it was pointless as I felt nothing supporting me. It would have felt weird if I hadn't already experienced what felt like a lifetime's worth of bizarre experiences over the past God knows how many hours.

I started to stew some sickly thoughts about what had just happened. Over and over again, my head played a horror film reel that depicted very graphic images of Jade all over Brad, and it filled me with rage. I even started to scream and swear but the sound was simply swallowed by the surroundings. I didn't even get an echo.

As my anger started to defuse, my thoughts returned to the failed exit plan. I hadn't been automatically thrust towards the exit; just like I hadn't been thrust into the next app like I tried earlier. No surprise there then. I knew that was probably a long shot. However, I didn't even get chance to reach out for any other avenues of escape. I was literally a slave to my phone's cruel intentions. How could I have been so stupid to think this would have been in any way helpful?

My situation was starting to seem a bit desperate now and it should have left me enduring a complete meltdown, but it didn't. I didn't even care anymore. It was at that point I lost all will to return to home. What was once an entrapment, suddenly seemed like a solitude in which I was safe from the pain and grief of the outside world. At that moment I was sheltered from hurt, numb to pain and cast away from real life.

It occurred to me that I was in a world without responsibility. No one cared what I looked like. I could exist in a world of endless possibilities without anyone around to give a damn. Who needs snake like people like Brad and Jade in your life anyway? Desperate to distract myself from the pain that tore through me, I decided to go on another virtual adventure in the small hope it might take away some of the anguish. But then I remembered, this world of endless opportunities wasn't actually endless at all, as I was restricted to two rows of apps, three at a push.

I had little time to build further frustration though because my phone seemed to sense my sudden thirst to explore and decided to empower me with a notification of someone's birthday. I barely knew the person whose birthday it was and don't recall ever even speaking to them, but little did they know they had provided me with the gift of opportunity. I was so thrilled I almost considered writing them a happy birthday message, but then I reminded myself that doing so would be weird.

Fortunately, I was transmitted to the top of the birthday message screen where there was a home screen logo within easy reach. This enabled me to navigate to the stream of social media activity, rather than being forced to write a message.

It was unusual to see the content I mind numbingly scrolled through every day on such a grand scale. I was immediately greeted by a mountain of bright, golden chips that were drowning in a variety of different cheeses. The projector size image glistened brightly like the sun and should have made my eyes water. It was captioned, 'Tag someone in this to make them hungry.' There was a huge white play button in the centre of the image, which was thankfully in easy reach now and I was able to scroll to my heart's content.

After playing the video, I was rewarded with the scene of a large silver ladle which unleashed a gushing waterfall of hot, steaming liquid gold, in a multitude of shades. Any normal person would have been salivating at such torture, but not me. I was entranced by the video but no longer felt hunger. My artificial new self clearly didn't require food to survive.

After the first video, I quickly became a slave to memes and surprisingly found myself in stitches as I watched videos of sausage dogs running around in hot-dog outfits, a bolshy couple playing pranks on each other and a compilation of unsuspecting individuals being hit with cream pies.

It wasn't long before I got lost in the stars. I embarked on a mindless journey through current snippets of my favourite famous family's life problems. I read an article about how Hannah was going to follow in her older sister's footsteps and get a boob job to get the attention of her man. The idea was crazy as her boobs were already massive. I was intrigued by her sister Zoe's comments however, which talked of how it helped transform her marriage to rap star Zane. I mean Zoe wasn't exactly a looker, but she seemed to have done well for herself with her beach-ball chest, pumped up lips and trim figure.

Throughout the article, oversized images of Zoe's breasts before and after were thrust into my face and found myself in stitches once more.

Time began to disappear into oblivion as my mind absorbed meaningless content like a porous sponge. Aside from the mountain of memes, celebrity gossip, fake news and God knows what else, it wasn't long until I found myself fixating on the updates much closer to home.

At first, I found myself casting judgement on a girl I knew from school who had posted an update about how her dad had bought her the most amazing dress for prom. Even though I knew my dad would probably do the same, I couldn't help but brand her as a spoilt little bitch as I radiated envy.

That was my first bite of the worm. Social media had cast its bait and I was stupid enough to get reeled in.

Next, I noticed that my mum had posted a picture of the meal that she tried to lure me into having, captioned 'great food, time for a few tipples'.

I was used to my mum posting awkward statuses like this and would usually cringe, but something about this one momentarily filled me with a warm feeling of home which was quickly punctured by a sick feeling and sadness that I hadn't gone. The food looked really nice too.

I forced myself to ignore the ludicrous feelings and then reminded myself that it was all her fault. If it wasn't for my parents, I could have gone to the party, Jade wouldn't have got with Brad and I wouldn't have found myself stuck in my smartphone!

I swiftly preceded to nosy on someone else.

The turmoil worsened after a scroll down to refresh the page invited an unwelcome status from Sammy, making my stomach lurch. It read, 'Looking like a cosy night in for one, with plenty of wine and a shit film. Feeling perplexed.'

It was another kick in the face, but I still couldn't convince myself I didn't deserve it, even considering my punishment so far. It was clear that dark clouds were forming around me and I needed to find a quick route out of this storm before I got swept away in a sea of depression. Then the answer came to me in the shape of a bright blue sky, crystal clear, sun drenched waters and lush green tropical trees.

It was an annoying reminder that my cousin Katie was still travelling with her husband-to-be. Not only was she spending a month travelling around all kinds of exotic locations, Thailand and Bali to name just a couple, she was forever posting pictures and videos to rub it in. This image was one of them both basking on what looked like their own private beach, with the hashtag 'paradise'. Hashtag nobody cares is what I say!

When I clicked on the first picture, I was transported to that very same paradise where not a cloud tormented the sky. I was stood on a cushion of lush white powder; not that I could feel it. The picture-perfect image looked so similar to my phone wallpaper, it was weird. Clearly this one hadn't been ripped from the web like mine was though.

A serene mixture of turquoise and clear-looking liquid stretched out as far as the eye could see and this was only disturbed by grand guardians of rock that rose up from the sea here and there, covered in plush, emerald green coats of dense jungle. This rich green landscape etched out to the far left and right of the picture frame, on each side protecting the haven within.

Slap bang in the centre of the frame stood my cousin, wrapped in a loving embrace by her fiancé. Her luscious brunette locks glistened in the sun's reflection and her freckled face was accompanied by a beaming smile that showcased her pearly-white teeth.

Six foot something Craig stood tall next to her but had casually relaxed his posture in an attempt to reach her level, allowing his lean looking arms to effortlessly cushion her waist. He was also sporting a full set smile, but one that looked like it could develop into laughter. The couple were freeze frame still, looking straight in my direction, presumably to whoever was taking the picture at the time.

It felt strange looking into a place that seemed so real but yet was only a snapshot in time. It made me realise that the ripples in the sea remained static. The green landscape ahead refused to sway in a light breeze that may or may not have occurred. A bird in full flight was also completely motionless in the canvas sky.

Regardless of the artificial make-up, I longed to explore this idyllic landscape further and so attempted to do just that. Tentatively, I tried to walk towards the picture-perfect couple. I was immediately stunned as the ability to walk freely was permitted. This ability was misguided however, as rather than enabling me to reach my destination, my imaginary footsteps instead triggered a zooming action on the image.

The swiftness of my excited footsteps quickly magnified the size of the two people, thus creating huge scale and slightly pixelated heads that towered before me. The result was both obscure and disturbing. It was too much for my eyes to handle and so I quickly backtracked, which allowed me to zoom back out to normal focus.

The bitter taste of disappointment choked me as the ability to fully embrace this luscious experience was once again denied.

Time to go back.

I knew I had to reach down for the button below, but I wasn't quite ready to return to the home page just yet. Katie had a stack of photos and videos from her time away and even though the first was somewhat disappointing, I longed to get another fix.

Having played this game for some time now, I was starting to become accustomed to the rules. I knew my phone offered me the option to return to the album and as I reached out to touch an imaginary screen, the back button offered itself to me in the bottom left-hand corner of the screen. Virtual logic also enabled me to figure out how to get there. I simply tilted my head upwards and started to walk.

I wasn't even that shocked when I found myself walking up across the imaginary sea and sky towards the glistening arrow of opportunity. As expected, the arrow transported me back to the album page in an instant.

Large image thumbnails flooded my immediate view. I found myself frantically scrolling through them to find something more exciting. I was irritated to find many similar beach shots of the two of them posing in different positions and perspectives; both together and separately. Suddenly I found one that emanated a little play button in the middle of the screen. This was of course a homemade video and I had every intention of diving in.

The phone bowed to my command and transported me back to beach paradise. However, this time I found myself effortlessly bobbing around in the tranquil water, gazing back towards the silky sands and idyllic landscape from which I had intruded just moments ago.

What was remarkable this time however is that I was a whole figure of myself, rather than being condensed into nothing more than the camera's restrictive eye.

I was able to move. I could see myself move in the water and I could even swim. And then there was the noise. It hit me like the sweetest of songs; the gentle lapping of the waves echoed in my ears. The delicate whisper of the breeze spoke so kindly to me, and then swiftly, the sound of splashing and laughter cut through the air. I quickly realised that my cousin was also bobbing around beside me, equipped with snorkel gear.

'Are you ready to be amazed, K?' questioned Craig, from what seemed like exactly where I was stood.

'Let's do this!' replied Katie whilst waving an enthusiastic thumbs up. 'I can't wait to see the little fishes.'

Craig laughed at her response and proceeded to tease her. 'Don't forget the sharks too?'

'Shut up, Craig, there's no sharks around these parts, the guide would have said!'

Sensing the note of panic in his fiancée's response, Craig quickly reassured her. 'I'm only joking, babe, I promise there won't be any sharks.'

'Right, let's go,' Craig quickly concluded, clearly in an effort to get cracking before Katie had a chance to dwell on the possibility of sharks and have a change of heart.

I abruptly found myself moving beneath the water as if I was being dragged alongside my cousin on a giant fish hook that was secured to my mouth, gently pulling me downwards towards them both, rather than out of the water by a fisherman. Although the movement was subtle and the view spectacular, I was irritated at being forced along like a dog on a leash.

After being forcibly submerged, I was greeted by an abundance of vibrant colours. Shoals of brightly-coloured fish in all kinds of shapes and sizes glided through the water in a multitude of directions. Katie and Craig were clearly in awe of what they saw as we all stopped to admire the underwater city.

The occupants were far from shy and I was stunned as the iconic orange and white stripes of a clown fish headed straight my way. In fact, within seconds it was just millimetres from my face. And just like that it was gone. I turned around and it was directly behind me swimming in the same parallel line. It had clearly swum through me, which reminded me once more that I didn't actually exist in this universe.

In fact, regardless of the sublime chaos of the natural wonders that surrounded me, I couldn't help but be distracted by the fact Craig was obviously filming and I was again taking the form of the camera eye view.

I just couldn't work out why I had so much more freedom this time though. I had a full 360-degree range of movement and could even see myself.

My brain was now rising from the boggy marsh of confusion though and as my thoughts stewed things over, it soon became quite logical. I only had a 360-degree scope of the camera, when the camera was being moved full circle by the beholder. My phone had taken another step in convincing me that I was right there in the moment. It was both remarkable but terrifying at the same time.

All the while this innovation had distracted me from the fact, I failed to feel the refreshment of warm tropical water on my skin, feel the light breeze enter my skin and let the warmth of the Asian sun ooze through my body.

Even though I was acting like a professional swimmer, I learnt that I was actually quite capable of walking around the immediate area when I stopped to try. How embarrassing that I hadn't tried this and worked it out already.

The worst thing was that I couldn't even get a response from my cousin who was in fact getting the whole experience rather than some weird imitation.

Regardless of all this, I had for some time, failed to even notice the essential life processes once more. The need to breathe underwater, for example, it just was not necessary. In fact, did I need to breathe at all for that matter?

In my mind I was breathing but was this actually happening? How had I not noticed this before? When was the last time my body dictated I breathe? I was starting to freak out again.

I tried to calm myself down by focussing on the serene surroundings, but then couldn't help but notice a dark-looking figure looming in the distance. It was getting larger by the second and just moments later it became frighteningly obvious what the figure was. I tried to scream out to Katie to warn her, but my bellows were fruitless.

At this point I found myself being strung along once more, but this time it was with much more urgency. Then, in a flash, all movement ceased, everything went black and in a split second I was back to the thumbnail screen once more.

13

VIRTUAL SICKNESS

I was suffocated by a savage attack of anxiety. What the hell just happened? Was that thing swimming towards us, really what I thought it was? Was my cousin ok?

I had to take an almighty swing back at the crippling anxiety and remind myself that Katie had to be ok or she wouldn't have posted the video. What if she or Craig had been injured though? What if the video was posted as a warning to others?

The couple were still away as far as I was aware. What if they were injured receiving treatment in some run-down hospital?

I had to get a grip! I tried to take a breath, but zero physical action occurred. This just compounded my disorientated state.

It then dawned on me that the best and probably only way to get a better perspective was to return to the dreaded video for clues. I reluctantly reached out ahead to press the video icon once more.

This time I realised that I had pressed the thumbnail twice the first time. This time, the one click simply enlarged the image; and thankfully it was captioned, 'The moment we had a lucky escape'.

I was flooded with relief; however, this was only short lived and was replaced by anger. How could Katie put me through that? The feeling of immediate danger had been so real and there had been nothing I could do about it. At the end of the day, the video was a memory and I should be ashamed of myself for getting caught up in it. Why was I acting so crazy?

This place was injecting me with a poison that sickened the mind; and I was acting like a chain smoker in need of another death stick. I was hard-wired to the phone like a marionette in a puppet show and offered myself freely to its every command.

As if waking from sedation, I was coming to my senses again. I reminded myself that it was time to find a way out of the phone for good! The task now felt urgent, I was like a soldier preparing for battle; I began to steer my mind solely on the job in hand. There would be no more holding back now, no more getting tangled in this cruel game anymore.

I reached as far down as I could, with purpose, in search of the big home screen button. In horror, the slightest of touches connected with the back button which instead took me back two steps to the social network stream from which I came. This left me staring at one of Katie's cover images for her holiday album which contained a deadly looking accumulation of dense and dark storm clouds that looked to be forming with angry intent in the distance.

Starting to feel apprehensive yet again, I tried to ignore this unusual set back and reached for the home button again. Terror abruptly gripped me as my actions failed once more. It seemed as though the touch screen had jolted towards me, thus sandwiching me into a situation where any movement forced me to scroll on the screen.

Even though I had been trapped in here from the start, it was only now I felt in any real danger. Only now did I feel I was being caged and tortured. Only now I could see no way to escape from this evil artificial reality.

The stream before me was now scrolling wildly and I found that my hand was unwillingly forcing this action. Upon realising my unsavoury possession, a renewed strength in me tried to fight it, but all I could do was make the scrolling momentarily stop. But it stopped on a sickening post captioned, 'Scientists confirm that the Earth will end this year'.

I found my eyes popping as they strained for what felt like a lifetime on each of the words like they were being tattooed onto my brain.

I knew I had to fight a powerful urge to click on the article. It would only fill me with further dread if I delved into the detail. Normally, curiosity would kill the cat and I would flick through horror stories like this one. They rarely offered joy or hope, two things I really needed at this moment.

As I tried to move once more, the scrolling continued, with even more intensity. It stopped again on another post that made my skin crawl. It read 'Rampant rapists target more children than ever before'. I had no choice but to endure the words presented to me. They made me feel sick and angry; enough to almost click and read more in the hope it would offer some kind of solution to tackling the revolting issue.

What the hell was I thinking? I needed to get out of here, and with that thought the phone scrolled down more wildly than before.

It stopped on an article captioned, 'World War Three imminent as world leaders collide.'

Again, I was forced to reach these horrific words of terror and they consumed me with yet more fear. This time I had no urge to click and read on, I just wanted out. I reached down to find my salvation, this time taking extra care not to lean forward too much; but I still lurched forward slightly too far and got punished as my head brushed the screen with the finest of touches. This prevented me from reaching the home button and the whole screen flashed violently, before spewing out another deadly article for me to digest. This one was captioned 'Addicted - are smartphones damaging our mental health?'

The words were chilling. How wickedly ironic they were, given my current circumstance. Behind the headline lurked a sinister message that was rammed down my throat to shed light on my sinful ways. I'm sure it was the obsession with my smartphone that got me in this mess. Why did I have to accept the invite from that weird Virtuality notification? If only I'd ignored the request, I would probably be at Sammy's now, munching on pizza and having a fab time. What I would do for that now.

I really did not want to linger on the deadly detail, but the phone had other ideas. I'm fairly certain that my hand was forced against the screen to unearth the lecture within. I can now see why the Americans call it a 'cell' phone. I was being held against my will and tortured by my captive.

My eyes worked like a bar code that scanned the words on the screen; I couldn't stop them as they ruthlessly monitored the data in front of me. The addiction article spewed all kinds of scary facts about how spending too much time on our screens impacts the chemical compounds within our brain, subsequently resulting in reliance and quashing our ability to function in everyday society.

The article prompted me to conclude what I've known for ages. I already knew I was addicted, but it had never seemed a big deal in the past. So what, I like using my phone. I had never caused any harm to anyone by it. I mean maybe it was a bit anti-social at times, but who cares. It wasn't until now that I entertained the idea that it may be harming my own health. In fairness, I think this realisation has been like a boiling kettle ever since I decided to sack Sammy off this afternoon. Since then, it has taken a new level of crazy to reach this place.

I had to remind myself that this was all a sick fantasy, made up; not real. I pushed these bad thoughts away and clicked back off the article and on to the never-ending social media storm. I had no choice but to prepare myself for another battle against the mass of public hate and thereafter, find a way to break free all together.

This time I very carefully pirouetted towards the elusive home button, which was surprisingly easy. Remarkably, I found myself just inches away from my holy grail and then a diamond in the rough caught my eye. Amongst the sea of nastiness was a suggested story, below what I had just read, captioned, 'Rohnan Blue to stage Charity gig at O2 arena'. This acted like a firework in my brain again and I found the torturous commotion that surrounded me melt away.

I didn't click on the article straight away. I simply glared at the thumb nail, entranced. All logic dictated that I should not click on that link. Although the tsunami of fear had washed away, a half-hearted voice in my mind was still trying to drag me away from further co-operation with the demon phone.

But it wasn't strong enough.

A voice of ill reason persuaded me that this article would be one last reward for enduring such stress, and so against my better judgement I clicked on it and was pleasantly surprised with what I read. It talked about how Rohnan had been strongly affected by what he saw in a recent visit to Africa for Comic Relief. It talked about the ongoing mission that help raise awareness of poverty issues and how the popular singer felt inspired to do something more about the situation. The article proceeded to talk about how live guests would also be performing and how funds raised would go to helping the hunger crisis. Details of the date and ticket sales followed thereafter.

See, that wasn't too bad, I told myself. If anything, it had me excited. Moreover, it had me hoping that all of this wasn't just a sick dream and this gig would actually be happening.

As I reached the bottom of the article, I realised that like most articles, a flock of individuals had commented on it. I couldn't help but get drawn in and after reading the first couple that emitted excitement, I clicked to see more ...

I was met with a mass stream of conversation and it wasn't long before I found one that was controversial. 'Clearly Rohnan is just putting this on for the extra attention, just saying.' The comment made me angry, but clearly not as angry as the respondent who replied, 'Is this some kind of sick joke? He's clearly doing something for a great cause and making a difference.' This was enforced by about six or more comments that were similar in nature, before someone else added another perspective. 'I like the way this is all blowing up #fishingforlikes.'

From here, things just seemed to escalate as vicious levels of savage back and forth arguments went on and on. I was never usually bothered by pesky trolls, but this time they had hit a nerve. What's more, I found that I was automatically scrolling through the screen once more as comment after comment was plastered into my skull.

The whirlwind of hatred twisted uncontrollably as people who were drunk on keyboard confidence battled to get their voice heard and slaughter their newfound enemies. The sheer intensity in which the arguments ensued was overwhelming and started to give me a headache.

The occurrence of a normal human sensation was a new development in what was a world of artificial chaos, but not a good one as it pulsed, burned and wounded me. As the concoction of agony penetrated, a small part of me realised that pain was good. Pain was human; pain was trying to keep me alive. Be that in this crazy version of living or the real thing, I had no idea, but my gut told me that the pain was positive.

It was finally becoming clear to me now that it was my phone obsession that had got me in this mess. I was human and I needed to start acting like one to beat this thing. This strength of humanity cascaded me to the home button and shielded me from the devious temptations of technology as I was able to reach down and find its solid presence. Like a superhero, it appeared in the nick of time and without delay I pressed it with force. The blackout came again and then there I was, back on the deceivingly calm-looking home screen.

14

THE RETURN

A naive part of me thought my actions would surely be all powerful and somehow release me from my cell this time. The experience so far should have taught me that this was wishful thinking. It was clear that to win I would need a clear mind, strong will and common sense. I had to be tough and do whatever it took in order to get back home.

My moment of empowerment was diverted in an instant as a loud ping shook the screen and introduced a familiar face, or should I say a fantasied copy of one. It was Jemma, the creepy emoji from earlier. Her unusual arrival sent a very real shiver down my spine. Amongst the carnival of crazy adventures, I had all but forgotten the strange wisdom of this... thing. As I stood there dumbfounded at her unnatural smile and slightly alien like stance, it became clear to me that this girl (if you could call it that) had a very real part to play in this whole experience.

Jemma stood square in the middle of the screen. She was much larger than when I saw her before, and this gave her an air of authority that was vacant during our initial introduction. She was still dressed the same as earlier, flaunting her odd-looking sandals and baggy dungaree combo, but something about her expression seemed more assertive this time.

If Jemma had noticed the shocked-looking glare I couldn't help but cast her way, she didn't show it. Before I had chance to speak, it addressed me.

'Hi Lindsey. So good to see you again!' she announced, as if our meeting was the most natural occurrence ever.

'Hi,' I offered, out of sheer politeness.

'I see you have been experiencing some of the many delights that your phone has to offer?' Jemma replied, swiftly moving on from the pleasantries.

Crippled with dread, I could only bring myself to nod in reply.

'It would seem as though you have achieved a lot. Done things you could only dream of, even.'

I didn't know if it was a question or an observation and so once again, I simply nodded to agree and Jemma's artificial smile from earlier was replaced with one that was hard to read.

'I can see from your journey you have learned much more about your phone than you ever imagined; this I'm sure of, would you agree?' she probed.

'Yes, I suppose so,' I confirmed, wondering how on earth Jemma knew the inner details of the journey I have had since we were introduced. Was this some kind of spyware that had tracked my every move? Most likely.

A moment of deathly silence followed, during which Jemma strolled casually to the left of the screen towards me. She then looked me up and down and simply extended her smile in my direction. The anxiety created by this move choked me and I prayed for her/it to leave.

'Would you say your opinion of this place has changed at all since we spoke earlier?' Jemma enquired energetically.

I was terrified at the thought of saying something wrong and being punished as a result. I wanted to just ignore her presence and continue with my escape mission, but I knew I had to offer something to her direct question.

Given my potentially grave set of circumstances, I had nothing to lose. Although Jemma could be a potential danger, it also occurred to me that this girl could be my only ticket out of here. I decided to tell her the truth and wished that by some miracle she was the key to my salvation.

I proceeded to tell her about the endless mind games I had endured over the past God knows how many hours I had been on lockdown in the phone and how I had been sucked into endless content without really having any choice in the matter.

'I just really want to get back home. Can you help me?' I pleaded.

There was no doubt this outcry left me vulnerable, but I didn't care. For the first time in ages, I felt brave. Relief also started to come when Jemma responded with sympathy. She nodded appropriately to acknowledge my pain. The dying embers of hope started to burn once again within me.

'Thank you for sharing this with me, Lindsey. I am certain that you are now ready.'

I waited desperately for her to follow this confirmation with some magic words. However, when Jemma simply went mute, it left me drowning once more.

'That's great,' I responded, trying to maintain Jemma's optimistic tone, 'but can you help me?'

Jemma beamed at me once more. 'You don't need any help from me now, Lindsey, you've had the ability all along. You just needed to learn a few lessons first. Don't worry, your path should be clear now and I'm sure you can sort things from here. I wish you the best of luck.' And in the time it took to blink, Jemma was gone.

Oh shit! I thought. Jemma had well and truly left me for dead. She had offered me wings and then savagely snapped them mid-flight.

What did she mean, I had the power to sort things from here? I had nothing but wild ideas that had got me nowhere. My anger towards this girl began to bubble like lava. I had no answer to Jemma's intervention, except she had simply appeared to taunt me about my torture in here.

I had to snap out of this little rage I found myself in. It wasn't going to get me anywhere and I needed to focus in order to 'prove Jemma wrong, or right' depending on how you looked at it.

I took a few moments to clear my head and focus on a new plan of action. I spent some time looking up towards the reset button. I could almost see a little slither of it sticking out slightly in the corner of the screen.

After what seemed like a lifetime of brain detective work, I was still at a loss at what to do. I was, however, feeling much sharper in my clarity of thought, which was actually making everything feel even more terrifying.

I noticed that the screen suddenly lost its overwhelming artificial glow. This bizarrely had the opposite effect and felt as though someone had wickedly flicked on a blinding light in the dead of night. It attacked my eyes with white-hot pain.

Everything on the home screen turned dull and lifeless, giving off just enough navigational spark for me to see a glum imitation of the phone's former self. I didn't even have to look up at the drained battery symbol and warning figure that read out my last rights of 15% to realise I was potentially in mortal peril.

15

BATTERY PROBLEMS

I found myself cast in the dark shadow of evil and started to gift all the symptoms of terror that the culprit of my nightmare quite clearly craved. Panic exploded out of me like volcanic ash. My thoughts were erratic, I could feel a heartbeat once more; and it was accelerating. It was becoming obvious that the end was near and there was nothing I could do about it.

14%

Not knowing what to do, I glanced again at the almost empty egg-timer of fate and felt a wave of sickness crash over me. I knew only so well that the moment my phone hits that 15% battery stage, the power starts to rapidly deteriorate. I couldn't be sure exactly how much time this left me with, but I know with absolute certainty it was not long. I had 10, perhaps 15 minutes max.

Even though I had lost all rational thought, I screamed at myself to do something. I wouldn't give in to what perilous end I might reach in here without doing something! The first sensible idea I conjured up was to bide some more time by any means necessary.

13%

As another glance hit me with this low blow, it was evident that I was losing grip fast; too fast. Then it was clear why. In fact, it was clear why I was hit with a dwindling battery in the first place.

I reached down and touched the left of the home button and a large thin backward arrow illuminated. I touched it again and at once a mountain of app pages, all neatly stacked, cast an accusatory glare down on me. Each had been lingering behind the scenes, sucking the life from me. I immediately began swiping them away, starting with the most recent social media screen, all the way back to the Balloon Trouble adventure which started this whole slippery slope. Each app that I swiped away enabled the next one to drop down in its place. This was very fortunate given my miniature state.

Putting a stop to my constant phone activity made me feel slightly better. Rather than being on the verge of a breakdown, I was now just in a serious state of panic.

Another glance confirmed that we were still on 13%, which gratefully confirmed the relentless pace had been laboured. This was a lifeline, but I knew it was only a slim one. I still needed to act fast.

I had to think solely on the phone's functionality. Unless there was a secret little hack that I didn't know about the buttons around me, I could say with absolute certainty that they wouldn't be able to help me. Think, Lindsey, think!

I looked around the home screen once more and was reminded of my earlier realisation that phones gave so many opportunities to connect with the outside world. It was cruelly ironic, but this time I was not laughing. When you think that no one in their right mind would take me seriously if I reached out as an animation in a smartphone, my current situation seemed dire. I could text, call, email or message through about a million social media apps. I had all the help I could ever want if anyone would just be open minded enough to believe me.

As crazy as it seems, I had to use the tools on offer and reach out to my mum. Even if it did sound beyond insanity, what was my alternative, death perhaps? I was running out of options and worse still, time to save myself.

This time I knew I had to think very carefully about how I approached the situation. I had one shot at this. If my plan didn't work, it was looking like game over. Stress heightened inside me as I strained my brain, pining for a solution that could work. I needed to come up with a logical plan whilst also making sure that I didn't spook my mum. If she freaked out or thought this was some kind of weird spam, she could easily cut me off and I would be doomed.

Everything around me continued to darken as I fought for an answer.

Finally, something in that remarkable brain of mine clicked. Rather than panic her with the truth I would message her on Socialise pretending to be at Sammy's using her computer as I had forgotten my phone. I could ask her to enter my room, reset my phone for me and put it on charge. It was very random and would raise some questions, but at the same time brilliant and so simple; I don't know why it took me so long to conjure it up.

As I continued to stew over the plan, it was clear that it could open a can of unworldly worms. My phone might not be there. Maybe it would be, and my mum would see me as an emoji, locked within a tiny home screen. Perhaps my phone would be a giant that overwhelmed my room. Worst still it occurred to me that my mum and dad had been out for a meal and they might still be. This dire realisation acted like an electric shock as it confirmed my bright spark idea was a massive long shot. But now wasn't the time for reservations. I had to pray that enough time had passed and they were now back home. I had no choice but to go ahead with the plan, and fast.

I plucked up all the courage I could muster and swiped reluctantly on the envelope icon once more, this time 100% ready to send a text. I thanked my lucky stars once more for the shortcut bar that lay gracefully in my eye line. An absence of this would most certainly have been my last chance to take control of my situation, as the only other means to communicate in within my reach was Emojime, and it was very rare that my mum would ever use the app or even notice a notification from it.

I clicked on to mine and my mum's message conversation. The immediate stream of family text was like an umbilical cord, that connected us just like they did at birth; and in this dark hour, I really needed this connection to trigger my mum's instinct to protect her young.

I couldn't help but choke on the last message I had received from my mum. It read, 'Cheer up, Linds. I hope you have a good time at Sammy's. Maybe we could go out for lunch tomorrow, just us. I will talk to your dad in the meantime about being so hard on you. See you later. Love mum x.'

Reading this filled me with everything from rage, frustration, and guilt. It made me hysterical and intensified my desperation. I don't even remember getting the message. I must have been so wrapped up in this crazy game, that it slipped through the net.

Come on Lindsey, get a grip; use this as a chance to put things right, you can't let mum's message get to you. I treated her so badly and it looks as though I've paid the price. What happened before was irrelevant now. I simply need to get out of this, in whatever way physically or virtually possible. I'd have plenty of time to make amends for my moody outbursts later.

Right, I had to start writing something. As I started to type, the screen drew another dying breath and slipped another shade darker.

12%

Another crucifying glance confirmed that the battery had sunk further towards its grave. I could hardly see what I was writing at this point.

If only I could just adjust the settings slightly to temporarily restore the brightness. And then it clicked. Of course, why on earth did I not think about this? I could surely reset the phone through my settings option. I almost cried out with joy at my own thinking. I felt like a lengthy drought was about to be quenched by girthy grey clouds.

'Don't worry mum, I will get myself out of this mess!' I shouted aloud.

I swiftly navigated my way back to the home screen and away from my mother's comfort. It was time to stand on my own two feet. Right, now think. How do I get on to settings?

In all the time I had owned a phone, and the endless hours spent being sucked into stupid games and pointless posts without barely giving it a thought, it was far too easy to miss the dreary, sensible, settings option. For a split second, I was terrified that it was out of reach, but then I could see it directly in my eye line. It couldn't have been much more accessible, but somehow its washed-out, complex-looking grey cog seemed to be smothered by the bright, bold, big hitters beside it. At that moment, however, it shone out to me like an angel from heaven.

Upon clicking on the phone's haven of wisdom, I was immediately overwhelmed with a sea of options, each sounding as uninspiring as the last. I started scrolling through the multitude of multicoloured requests, sifting through jargon-riddled buttons such as mobile hotspot and tethering accessibility. I didn't have a clue what either of these options meant or what they did, but they didn't immediately scream reset to me. Time was slipping away fast and I didn't fancy trying either option on the off chance.

There was no immediate reset option, but of course there wasn't. Why would there be? I started to question whether there even was a way to reset. Maybe it had to be done manually. After some quick deliberation I had narrowed down my further search to check either 'control centre' or 'general'.

I opted to look at 'control centre' first. It was immediately clear that this was the wrong option. I was dealt the joker card, as only two options were given; one called 'Lock screen override' and the other 'Application access'. The fact I didn't even know what either of these options meant, frustrated me.

10%

My phone's battery once again cried out its pending exhaustion; and this time it did so with a dire warning message. The words 'Extremely Low Battery' were cautioned across the screen and I knew I had little time to question what was an obvious misdirection and so returned back to the settings home screen.

Just as I began my quest for the 'General options' escape plan, the hands of fate took one final turbulent turn.

A Socialise message engulfed my screen. Its contents diverted my attention in an instant. Its grave message was frightful: 'Not that you probably even care, but I think it's time I left this world behind. I don't fit in around here and doubt I ever will. The few people who have ever been a friend to me, only did it because they felt sorry for me. I just thought I would say goodbye. I hope you find happiness, I just hope it won't come in the next life, like mine.'

The sender was Sammy and it plunged me into an ocean of terror. My thought processes had gone haywire. It was as if my brain had been hacked by some sort of vicious virus; every attempt at making any kind of decision resulted in an annoying error message. Only one thought continued to shake me by the shoulders and scream in my face, I must do something to save her!

Sami's message had stolen another 3% of precious battery life ...

7%.

I was moments away from empty. I had to do something. My actions had to save at least one life. It was time to be brave, time to fulfil my final purpose. I opened a message to respond. What the hell could I say to prevent this tragedy? Think, Lindsey, think.

The only thing that seemed powerful enough to have an impact would be to knock down the walls I had built around me and come clean as much as I could; somehow without telling her about my far from believable reality. Here goes nothing.

'Hey Sammy, I'm so sorry I didn't make it tonight, I really am. Please hear me out before you do anything! I'm not going to come up with any excuses for my actions today or any other day for that matter. All I know is that you are and have always been my only true friend; I don't know what I would do without you. You've always been there for me, but I've never treated you the way you deserve. There is an amazing life for you out there and you will find much better friends than me, believe me! Stay strong babe, I love you, your family loves you and the world needs you!'

There was no need to edit my words. It's surprising how little thought is required when it comes from the heart. The weight of the world had been lifted from my shoulders. I felt relieved, liberated even.

4%

Sending the message had accelerated the flooding in my sinking ship, meaning the time for drowning was near.

For a moment, I was willing to accept my fate with bravery and pride, but then the question of 'what if' kickstarted my human instinct to fight death one more time. My heart pounded like a drum and my whole body shook, but my brain worked like a steam train as it desperately fought to find an emergency cure.

I reached the settings functionality within seconds. I scrolled down to general and pressed it.

2%

The phone let out one last dying screech and shutter. Frantically I scrolled down the screen and at the bottom of the page the golden ray of hope welcomed me with life. Holding my breath, I moved in for the reset to end it all. Like flicking off a switch in the dead of night, darkness embraced me.

16

REALITY

Like a battered boat gently lapping up a tranquil shore after weathering a great storm, I gradually felt the wholeness of reality breathe into me again. I felt the warmth of cotton sheets caress my body. I could feel the strain of muscles as my arms and legs slowly navigated slightly around my immediate area. I was heightened to the flow of cool breeze that my lungs happily guzzled and released.

I was back in my room, back in my bed and everything looked exactly as it had been before I had left. I noted that I was still wearing my clothes that I had been wearing both in the real and not so real world, but nothing appeared to be unsettling about them. Everything seemed so still and quiet, but most definitely real.

I felt slightly disorientated, as I imagine it would feel awaking from a long coma. I slowly eased myself out of the bed and touched everything I could to confirm it was solid and real. I headed towards my window and looked out to find little had changed from what was presumably the night before; or at least I hoped it was only time that had passed. All the other houses in our horseshoe-shaped close looked perfectly normal; most of which had cars parked on the drive exactly as I remembered the last time I had seen them. I couldn't be 100% sure though and needed more evidence to prove it was in fact Sunday morning.

The sun looked to be slowly surfacing, offering a brilliant warmth through my window. This, along with the fact there seemed to be little life around, suggested the hour was early. This provided a stark reminder that I was always usually awoken by my phone. At this point, I would be robotically informed of the time. I had to ask the question about my demonic phone.

There it was, sitting innocently on the table to the side of my bed. I approached it with great trepidation. I closed in on it like I was about to dismantle a bomb, but it just looked like a normal phone. There was no relentless flashing light to inform me of pending notifications and a quick press of the home button and a palpitation to go along with it, confirmed it was dead. This was relieving news. As much as I needed to know what time and day it was, I just needed to stay away from that thing. I would find this information out by any other means!

My mind was now starting to fully awaken, and I instinctively demanded to know if my parents were home and if they were ok. If I had been gone for much longer than what the phone led me to believe, they would be worried sick. They might even be out searching for me. It then occurred to me that my phone was still here, exactly as I left it. Surely my parents would have used this to assist in their quest if I had gone missing. The thought was reassuring, but I wasn't out of the woods yet.

I practically sprinted out of bed and then across the hall to my parents' room. I came to an abrupt halt outside their door, which was closed. I could quite clearly hear my dad's harmonic snoring, which was sweet music to my ears. I decided not to disturb them unless it was necessary. After all, my whirlwind of horrors was most likely a dream. How could it not be? I just needed to confirm the time and date.

In my absolute certainty not to trust my phone again, I proceeded to the kitchen which was equipped with a digital clock on the microwave which boasted time and date options. The time read 7.30am which after a moment of reflection seemed logical and then a toggle through the settings fully assured me as it read 22.03.2015, the morning after my night of horrors.

A moment of euphoric relief caressed me as I slumped down on the breakfast bar that protruded at the end of the kitchen. I just sat there for a moment in a thoughtless daze, just absorbing my real-life surroundings.

After a gratifying few minutes, my thoughts returned to reflection on the events that may or may not have unfolded the night before. This forced a new wiry knot in my stomach as thoughts of the correspondence between myself and Sammy showed their monstrous claws once more.

I was pretty sure it had all just been a torturous nightmare, but the element of uncertainty crippled me. I had to know that Sammy was ok. In fact, I had to go and see it for myself and with that I bolted upstairs, threw on some jeans, a T-shirt and a hoodie and headed like a woman deranged to the front door, ready for a 20-minute mission to Sammy's estate; my phone left peacefully untouched still on my side table.

As I rapidly approached my front door, it suddenly occurred to me that my parents would wonder where I had gone, especially without my phone. Assuming something unusual did happen last night, this disappearance would not likely help the situation.

After a moment's contemplation, I decided to write them a note. Mum always had a pad a paper in the living room drawer, presumably for moments like this.

'Just nipped out to Sammy's. Phone playing up so left without it. Will be back later x,' I fired across the paper.

Even after reading it back several times, I knew it would raise more questions than answers, but I had little time to dwell on it. They just needed to know I was safe, and I needed to know Sammy was! There was no more hesitation and I bounced out of the house, my one aim to reach Sammy's house as quickly as possible.

17

SALVATION

Fuelled by actual real-life adrenaline, I sprinted out of the house. However, it wasn't long at all before my feeble fitness levels failed me and I had to stop and gasp for air like a stuffed old hoover; I had only made it a few streets away from home. I thought about getting the bus, but then realised it was Sunday and they wouldn't be running for another hour or so. Moreover, I had forgotten my purse in my sudden haste.

Alert to the fact Sammy could still be in grave danger, I knew I had to keep up the pace, regardless of the pain. I opted for a power walk, followed by short sprint bursts and an inevitable scream from my lungs as they tried to cope. This was so much harder than running on the digital map, but the human pain and brisk air was bliss in comparison to feeling nothing at all. I really did regret having all those cheeky fags behind the school sports hall though.

After what seemed like an eternity of dodging dog walkers, runners and unexpected cars, I could see Sammy's new build estate come in to view. At this point, I was soaked in sweat and I opted to secure my hoodie around my waist, about half a mile back. I really did underestimate the distance; it always seemed so close when my dad dropped me off. Although he used to take me reluctantly and always drove like a mad man.

I decided the rest of the short journey would be quickly consumed by a steady jog, but as I reached her house I broke out into a wild sprint, fuelled by a second shot of adrenaline. Sammy's driveway was the finishing line and I had no choice but to keel over and wretch as I reached my goal. I only stopped for a moment though as the danger was still very real. I was still panting excessively as I rang the doorbell.

After what seemed like an eternity, there was still no answer. In contrast to the blissful Sunday morning quiet that surrounded Sammy's street I was consumed with panic and found myself frantically calling the bell again and again. I felt light-headed as I awaited the hands of fate. Time had been frozen by hell itself as it punished me with one final torturous lesson. I was about to endure the dire consequences of being a terrible friend. What if Sammy has been true to her terrifying threat to end things? I just don't know what I would do. Come on, someone please answer the damn door!

I eventually heard footsteps that thundered louder and louder towards my direction. I was unexpectedly gripped with fear that Sammy's well-built dad would lunge through the door straight for my throat and choke me in a wild fit of rage to punish me for pushing his only daughter over the edge. I could see his towering outline accelerate towards me and the door crashed open with vigour before me.

'Can I help you?' demanded a disgruntled-looking man called Rob in his early 50s.

Rob looked flush from being suddenly alerted and was still wearing a dressing gown which was wrapped tightly around him. After a double take, he recognised it was me and instantly eased his assertive demeanour.

'Oh, it's you Lindsey.'

Rob's heightened state was now replaced with a look of confusion.

'What are you doing here at this time on a Sunday? And have you been running?'

My mouth went suddenly very dry as I knew I had to ask the words. Rob looked relaxed so surely nothing untoward could have happened.

'Yes, I was just seeing if Sammy was ok, she hasn't replied to my texts,' I lied.

Why did I have to put it like that? Rob looked taken aback and slightly perplexed.

'Oh right, erm I think so, I haven't heard a peep from her since last night. She's been sulking in her room. Let me just shout her down.'

'Sammy, Lindsey's here for you. Come and answer the door!' he shouted.

This was it. What if she didn't answer, what if she couldn't? What if I'm too late and we all find out the sinister truth together? The tension was unbearable; like the moment before charging into a bloody battle.

After a few moments in which Sammy failed to surface, I could tell a twinge of concern had been injected into Rob and my brow started to sweat once more. Come on, Sammy, get your ass down the stairs, I pleaded to myself. And then like a sloth slowly surfacing from a grand splendour of branches, Sammy meandered to the top of the stairs, stopped for a moment and then casually took the stairs towards us.

'Sorry I was just getting ready,' defended Sammy to us both, but mainly her disgruntled looking dad, who let out an exasperated sigh and wandered off back into the house and upstairs, back to bed presumably, mumbling something about troublesome children to himself along the way.

I felt dizzy with delight. It was like finding a paradise in the most desolate of deserts. A ten-tonne truck had been lifted off my shoulders. I found myself assessing Sammy before saying anything, just to make sure there was no visible signs of self-harm. She passed the test but looked at me like I was alien or something.

'Are you ok?' she enquired. 'What are you doing here so early? Did you text me because nothing's come through on my phone?'

Sammy's questioning seemed irrelevant to me and I just wanted to probe her to check she was ok. I realised that in doing so would be weird and potentially confirm the reality of last night's phone trauma that I was determined did not happen! So, I just stood and pondered what the hell to say that would sound like a plausible explanation. I felt too exhausted and liberated to really care so much and so just winged it and hoped she would buy into my explanation.

'Oh, I just thought I would come and apologise for not coming around last night. I'm really sorry I fell asleep stupidly early and then only woke up in the middle of the night, can you believe?'

'I woke again at like 6am, I couldn't get back asleep and knew my dad wouldn't give me a lift so thought I would go for a run and come knock on for you.'

Sammy looked at me with apprehension and then amusement as I reeled off my floundering speech. I waited for her to cut through my lie at any moment, but it never came. I longed to know the implications of her reactions, but I was too scared to find out for sure. I then waited anxiously for her to open up about her suicidal message, but thankfully it never came. In fact, she seemed totally normal and satisfied with what I said, which was good enough for me; the end of a long-twisted nightmare. Desperate to return to normality as soon as possible, I put an end to the explanation talks.

'Shall we have a mooch to the park?' I asked.

'Yeah, sounds good,' replied Sammy with enthusiasm and a look of relief.

With that we mindlessly wandered towards the park and it wasn't very long before we were back to our old ways. It was refreshing to have a bitch about, well, literally everything, but I automatically turned my attention to Brad and Jade after a pretty short time and then remembered the vicious scene I had endured the night before and then chose my words carefully in case it raised questions about what I had really been up to last night.

'I hope Brad had a shit time and that Jade, I can't stand her anyway,' I seethed.

I half expected Sammy to gossip about the specific live video from the party that I had been part of, but thankfully she didn't.

Still terrified that I might blurt out something which would force Sammy to confirm last night's reality, I tried to keep all further conversation related to last night's events, off limits; which given how much had gone down (real or not), was not easy.

After a while I started to relax a little bit more and was relishing the prospect of just chilling in a nice natural space, away from any technology. Without warning, my blissful reality was punctured once more, in the shape of a giant billboard at the side of the dual carriageway we were currently walking alongside.

This giant demon depicted a guy in his late teens or early 20s, bound by an enormous, tinted headset which enveloped his whole head. It included a sinister caption that read, 'Your invitation to a limitless reality is here'.

I immediately felt faint. How could I not see, what I experienced last night is really happening. It all made perfect sense to me now. What happened last night wasn't real, and neither are these headsets, not really. Were these devices really so different from what I endured last night? I had to snap out of this paranoia. I tried to convince myself that these VR devices were just that, virtual and not real. Further still, the virtual reality I found myself held captive in, was also virtual; albeit in the form of a vivid nightmare. It had to be. It can't have been real!

As much as I tried to contain my anxiety towards the sign, I found myself almost sprinting away from it, as though it was a vicious snake trying to attack.

'What are you running for?' enquired Sammy with a look of concern.

I literally had no explanation and my brain was in a deep freeze from terror.

'Erm I was just ... just trying to stretch my leg. I think I might have cramp.' I responded.

Sammy just looked at me and laughed.

'Ok then,' she said with amusement.

Nothing else provoked me as we reached the park and I

started to chill out again. As we entered the grand, green space, I felt liberated. It consisted of about an acre of lush, mowed greenery with grand oak trees, winding footpaths all surrounding a lake which was equipped with sausage-like reeds, and an assortment of birds. The occasional dog walker or jogger could be seen tearing up the pathways with purpose.

We decided to walk around the outskirts of the park and then make our way to a courtyard which was dotted with benches, wild flowers and secluded by trees.

'Isn't it great just to get out in the fresh air and not think about much else?' I asked Sammy.

'Yes, I suppose it is,' she replied with a reflective smile.

We both just sat there soaking up the sun, which was getting strong as we approached mid-morning. Before long, the inviting spring conditions started to draw people in through the park gates and when I eventually woke up from my dazed sense of serenity, I noticed that the courtyard was amass with people sat here there and everywhere, all enjoying the sun.

Then I noticed something else which made me feel crippling dread once more. Everywhere I looked, people were chained to their phone screen. It looked like a scene out of some kind of zombie apocalypse, watching an army of lifeless souls with limp heads trapped in their own addiction. How had I never noticed this before? I had an overwhelming urge to bark a warning to them all, but then I knew that my logical thinking would be deemed odd and potentially harmful. A feeling of helplessness wounded me.

It seemed as though humanity had become a slave to their own inventions, and I tried with all the strength I could muster to block out thoughts of this bleak-looking future reality for mankind.

As the sea of lifeless phone prisoners failed to show any signs of human life, except for the odd moment of (what seemed like) forced conversation, I just felt sick and decided it was time to leave the park.

'Shall we get moving?' I questioned urgently.

She seemed a bit startled by my sudden haste to leave but agreed.

'We could head back to mine for a bit for lunch if you want?' I added to sweeten the deal.

'Yeah, sure, that sounds like a plan.'

No sooner had we vacated our seats, we were greeted with a bloodcurdling scream from the path beyond the courtyard, just a few metres across from us. It quickly became clear that a guy dressed in what looked like running gear had just collapsed and there was an imminent emergency. A middle-aged woman with short salt and pepper hair had obviously been quick to spot the peril and had knelt down at the side of him.

'My name is Pam and I'm here to help. Can you hear me at all?' the woman pleaded to the man in jeopardy.

Sickeningly, there was no response and the helping woman looked frantic.

'He's not breathing,' Pam screamed in panic.

She then patted desperately around her pockets in search of her phone but failed to find it.

'Can somebody call an ambulance?' she bellowed into the courtyard.

By now, everyone had become alert to the situation and some acted crazy with apprehension whilst others unbelievably shied away from the drama, clearly pretending to be oblivious to the emergency. Funnily enough, it was primarily those chained to their phones who remained that way.

A young woman who must have been only a few years older than me was the first to rush over to Pam in an effort to help. Her phone became rapidly glued to her ear and I could hear her demanding for an ambulance to be sent. Then, unbelievably, Pam turned her attention away from the man and continued to pat down her pockets in search of a phone, which seemed like strange behaviour to me, seen as someone else was already hounding down the emergency services. After an agonising rummage, she located it in the back pocket of her jeans and looked relieved. She then started staring intently at her phone screen for what seemed like a lifetime. I couldn't believe what I was witnessing. A guy was between life and death here. Maybe she hadn't noticed the young woman coming over to help, or maybe she didn't trust her to. I don't know what was going on, all I knew is that I needed to help, and without thinking I found myself charging over towards the living nightmare.

Meanwhile, the young woman seemed rooted to the spot with a vacant expression plastered across her face. She stuttered and floundered in her attempt to explain the details of the danger to the emergency services. I could just about overhear her confirm her name as being Imogen, but she did so without conviction. Clearly, shock was starting to set in.

As the scene came into better view, it was apparent that the man in trouble was only young. He must have only been in his late 20s or early 30s and looked lean, with thick blond hair and light stubble. His vacant expression, however, terrified me.

Although Pam's initial intentions were noble, my wild rage towards her sudden stupidity was about to explode and then I realised that she was pleading with herself to understand the instructions for CPR. What an absolute idiot I was. Of course, she was determined to still help whilst we waited for the ambulance! Instead of going crazy, I found myself offering Pam my assistance.

'Is there anything I can do? Is he still not breathing?' I enquired nervously.

Pam looked thankful for my presence.

'Yes, please. I don't think he is.'

'I have some instructions for CPR here, but I have no idea if it will work,' she stuttered with fear.

In the background, I could hear Imogen had managed to communicate the essential information of our location, but this seemed to have exhausted her ability to help any further as she shut down, proclaiming she couldn't and didn't understand what I assumed was a command to try immediate lifesaving actions on the victim. The shock of the situation had clearly taken over and it was now down to us. I had a split second in which to either grab the phone from the woman and speak to the medics myself or read out the instructions. I went for the latter but bellowed at Imogen to stay on the phone in case things went south.

'It's ok, I will read them out step by step for you, if you want to try?' I offered to Pam.

She looked empowered by the help.

'Yes, let's do it. What choice do we have?' she replied nervously.

From there on in, I found myself being skilfully navigated through each intricate step by Pam's smartphone. I told her when to use compressions, when and how to breathe into the airway and how to check for a response. At this point, Imogen managed to get it together enough to return to the scene and put her phone on speaker phone. This enabled me to shout at the operator what we had tried so far and in turn the operator encouraged and corrected us as Pam applied pressure to the man's chest.

At first, nothing was working, but the phone operator prompted us to keep calm. I could feel sweat developing on my brow and I felt like my heart was about to throw in the towel too. Like two women possessed, we soldiered on in desperation and after what felt like a lifetime, the guy aggressively gasped and spluttered for air and coughed profusely. I couldn't believe it. We, completely normal, non-medically trained people, had managed to save this man's life, albeit with some eventual help from the professionals, by following instructions that were immediately available on a phone.

The next five minutes were spent comforting the man we learned was called Ryan, who was deeply confused about how he had ended up on the floor in the middle of the park. Pam helped to keep everyone calm with reassuring talk, whereas Imogen was still frantic with the shock and continually declared that Ryan could have died because of her. In a plea to avoid any further distress to the victim, I ushered Imogen away from the scene and tried to calm her down. When the ambulance staff arrived, they thanked us deeply for our lifesaving actions, but insisted they take it from here. I insisted that they see to Imogen as she seemed distressed, which they thankfully obliged and also took her into their care.

It was at this point I realised I was still holding Pam's phone. I just stood and looked at it for a few moments in awe. I then gave it back to her and walked away, realising in that moment everything had become clear.

18

TEN YEARS ON

Looking back at the days that followed the escape from my phone nightmare, it is crazy to think how terrified I was about the thought of using my device again. It took me several days to pluck up the courage to even turn it on. The possibility of awakening the savage beast once more felt incredibly real at the time. My heart raced for the entire few minutes of dread as I waited for it to spring to life. It didn't help that my nerves were still shot from the dramatic events that transpired in the park a few days earlier.

Thank goodness it all turned out to be fine. My phone innocently rebooted, exactly as it should. I wasn't plunged into anarchy.

It took a few more days before I would really use it with purpose. At first, I could only muster the courage to take baby steps. It was very much back to basics; for example, I would quickly look at the time or send a brief text.

It took years still before I could really use any kind of phone with ease and after what I went through, I was grateful for my phone upgrade and now any phone I do own, I use both sparingly and responsibly. In fact, the events of that mystifying night and the carnage that followed thereafter inspired me to educate others, mainly children, about the healthy usage of technology.

Now, at the age of 26, I actually own a small tech firm; ironic, I know. It turns out that, aside from being obsessed with my phone, I went on to understand everything about it. Maybe it was my own weird way of trying to rationalise the events of that harrowing night.

Even now I can't help but allow my thoughts to become smothered by the sickening memories of helplessly trying to conjure up an escape from my technology cage. These thoughts seem to have returned quite vividly today and I can only assume it is because I am in fact on the way to my office this afternoon for the launch of our most exciting but nightmare-inducing business project yet. Myself, along with my small team and a few technical wizards, have designed an app to teach individuals about the pros and cons of smartphones and signs that they are interfering with healthy everyday living. We wanted to capture the target audience right at the source. This is our most innovating idea yet and I just hope that people will embrace it.

Although the events of that night sparked this new passionate purpose in life, I eventually accepted the scary experience was nothing more than a psychological episode, most likely triggered to help me realise how addicted I was to my phone. In spite of how dangerously real it all seemed, it was just a figment of my imagination, of which the only lasting scar is inspiration.

At first, I was both distraught and wild with fear as Brad and Jade did get together about two weeks after the party in which I was subjected to the torturous live video. However, I could find no trace of the live video online or anywhere else for that matter.

I became obsessed with trying to find out the truth about the events of the party that I had endured but was shot down by everyone involved who were all adamant that nothing happened between the two.

I hounded the culprit – bolshy Becky - from the live video at the party I had been part of, who looked at me as though I was crazy and declared that she didn't even take any videos at the party. After several relentless attempts to break the girl and probe her about her misdemeanours around Jade's house, I had to accept defeat, as she threatened to report me to the police for harassment and said I needed to seek professional help. The more I thought about it, if the live video had made it online, the naked image of Brad and Jade would surely have gone viral.

Then there was the dreaded message from Sammy. How could I ever forget about that? If only Sammy would have sent this blood-curdling threat via standard messaging I would have had a definitive answer to my torment. Agonisingly, she decided to do the deed over the Socialise app. Unlike other messengers, this one conveniently wipes clean your conversation stream as soon as you exit the app. I guess this feature was built in to promote privacy; perhaps the exact reason why Sammy opted to open up to me in this way. The only way I could restore the message (if there even was one) was to approach the app helpdesk. At which point, they may have been alerted to the message and all hell could have broken loose.

When I could find no news about the Rohnan gig I had read about that night, or any evidence of other content I had endured, I knew I had to move on as the whole thing was causing me overwhelming stress and was taking a strangle-hold of my life. Why continue on a desperate hunt to find something that would only cause me pain and more than likely, didn't even occur.

After many years of fighting my demons, I finally came to my psychological episode conclusion. I accepted my mind had simply chosen to scare me with the most terrifying of realistic dreams. Rather than torturing myself with the past, I focussed all attention on my career. I bit the bullet and went to study ICT at college, then Business and Digital Design at University. I figured this was the only way to prove that phones were not in fact mystic monsters like I believed. During all my time of study (and thereafter in fact) I am yet to experience any evidence that phones are capable of what felt so real on that night. Since then I've never looked back.

After graduation, I managed to get some experience working for a big tech firm whilst working part-time in retail, before dad gifted me the Holy Grail to a bright new future. He kindly offered me a big investment so I could start my own tech firm. I couldn't believe it. Even though we haven't always seen eye to eye, I now know he always had my best interests at heart, and I will be forever grateful for his help on my journey. Today is the day I will hopefully reap the rewards for making a change and working like a Trojan since leaving my sinister school days behind me. It is time to prove that dad was right to have faith in me and repay him for the support.

Before I make my way to the launch, I have agreed to meet with Sammy for lunch in one of our favourite spots, as she apparently has some exciting news. It is going to be a good day, I just know it.

I'm in such great spirits as I drive to meet Sammy. On my way I can't help but ponder what the big news is. A year after the incident at the park where I had to instruct CPR, Sammy met a guy called James whilst at college and they've been inseparable ever since. What's more, he popped the question whilst on a trip to Paris last year and since then, I've never seen her so full of life.

Although I'm pretty content living the single life and taking hold of my career, I couldn't help but feel a twinge of jealousy about it all. However, I am truly happy for her; it's what she deserves. So, I conclude, the news can't be to do with that and I'm now scratching my head to figure out what this big news has to do with me. Maybe she's pregnant?

I'm literally giddy with excitement as I reach our eating spot, a quaint little café just outside town that backs on to a serene canal way. The place is a cottage which stands alone, half-way down a country road. It is the ideal place to escape from the bustle of town but is conveniently only a ten-minute drive away.

I don't need to check my phone to realise that Sammy had already arrived, as her light blue Fiat is already parked up outside. I carefully park my sparkling new Audi alongside her car, which takes some concentration as the car park is tiny and almost full.

A glance at my messages confirms that Sammy has already got us some seats outside around the back. This suits me fine as the spring sun is shining superbly right now.

I decide to walk the back route to the café, breathing in the sweet scent of blossom trees as I go. As I open the rustic farmyard-looking gate, I notice Sammy sat across the way, equipped with a large pot of tea. She beams at me enthusiastically upon noticing my arrival.

'Hey babe, you ok?' she questions as I take a perch alongside her.

'I'm really good, hun, thank you,' I answer sincerely. 'How about you?'

'Yes, I'm great Linds, it's really good to see you. It seems like ages since we last met up.'

In reality, it had only been about a month since we last met but seeing as we were so close it seemed like an age.

We spend the next ten minutes or so sipping tea and chit chatting about work, men, and old times.

It isn't until our afternoon tea assortment arrives that the true purpose of Sammy's invitation becomes clear. I can sense a slight shift in her demeanour as I hastily gorge on mini sandwiches and sausage rolls, desperately trying to block out thoughts of weight gain.

Sammy suddenly seemed fidgety and nervous.

'You ok, hun?' I enquire.

'Yeah fine, fine. I guess I should just come out with it ... the reason why I invited you here,' she responds without looking in the slightest bit fine. 'Ok, here goes,' she adds. 'I just wanted you to know how much you mean to me.'

'Aw, you too babes,' I respond, not quite sure where this is going.

'I'm serious, I've never had a friend who is so understanding and who's been there for me like you have.'

I look at her, even more confused.

'And that's why I want you to be my chief bridesmaid.'

I am overwhelmed with happiness at her request.

'Aw wow, I would love to. It would be an absolute privilege.'

I'm flooded with tears of joys as I reach over to embrace my best friend, then she adds more. 'I couldn't think of anyone I would trust more than you, Linds. I think it's time now after all these years to talk about the night of Jade's party.'

My blood instantly turns to ice. An endless and evil silence suffocates the moment.

'You know, the time when I was a complete nutter and talked crazy about ending it all?' Sammy concludes.

Sami was desperately trying to make this sinister blast from the past sound like it was all some silly moment of madness. Little did she know the horrifying implications that this revelation suddenly conjured up.

'I know both of us have never mentioned it again to each other after those messages and maybe it's because we were both scared about facing it. I just want to know that if it wasn't for your kind words in that text message, I might have done something silly and I wouldn't be here right now, as happy as a girl can be.'

I'm literally numb with shock and feel suddenly nauseous and light-headed. My brain is acutely reminding me that this is a tender moment and I need to respond appropriately, but I'm literally paralysed with dread.

'Are you ok, Linds, you look a bit pale?' Sammy questioned, looking guilty. 'I shouldn't have brought it up, should I? It was stupid of me. What's in the past is in the past.'

I know I need to reassure her that this has nothing to do with her.

'No, no, it's not that at all. I just feel a bit sick that's all, think I ate those sarnies too quickly.'

I force a very unnatural-sounding laugh, trying desperately to keep it together and act normal.

'I'm so proud of you, Sammy, for staying strong. I can't tell you how relieved I am that my words helped so much, as I don't know what I would have done without you.'

Then like the sudden bursting of a pipe, I spontaneously

erupt into tears. I don't know if they are born out of fear or out of emotion towards the friend I saved, or both, but they help to make me feel better somehow. This sets Sammy off too. We must look like a right pair, openly wailing in a little café which is full of people, but an audience is the last thing on my mind right now.

We continue to open up and talk about how much we need each other, but I dare not link it into the phone events which started to feel frighteningly more real by the second. Thankfully, conversation soon becomes centred about my duties as chief bridesmaid and it gives me a slight window to push aside my twisted phone thoughts.

After another half an hour, several more cups of tea and a few cupcakes, Sammy and I eventually part and then I'm left alone, with only my poisonous thoughts for company. I literally have to run to my car, as the clouds had gradually crept up on us as we went through the full range of emotions, but mainly terror on my part at Sammy's staggering news, and the heavens decide to open. The overwhelming emotion should have been happiness at Sammy's actual news at being gifted the honour of chief bridesmaid, but the suicide message confession consumed any feelings of joy and cast a darkness, darker than the stormy sky outside over me.

I sit behind the wheel staring absently ahead, swamped with questions about the revelation I had just endured. My phone abruptly starts buzzing wildly in my pocket and it immediately fills me with terror. It was of course a much newer phone than the one that did the damage; I had to get rid of that a few weeks after the event as I could never properly overcome the fear of a possible round two. Nonetheless, in a blind panic, I erratically throw it on the passenger side floor. After a few rings it goes dead and nothing crazy happens; it was acting like any normal phone does. I knew it would only be the developers wondering what time I would make it to the office for the launch. Our lunch turned out to last an unexpectedly long time.

Hands still shaking, I turn on the engine and take in a few deep breaths. I then start driving, my automatic wipers violently deflecting the pounding raindrops which try to penetrate the glass. I have to force my attention on to the road, rather than of that night, as I know the conditions demand it. The drive to the office is only a ten-minute journey but it seems to take me much longer today and I have a crushing headache by the time I arrive.

My office is situated on an open plan business park with lots of other little neighbouring offices all equally taking advantage of the cheap rent. I have a car parking space outside our humble habitat, but decide to park at the back of the car park behind other parked cars.

I need some more time to absorb what had just happened and I don't want to be spotted by the developers who are already impatient about the launch. Flashbacks of me throwing coloured spears and being made to constantly scroll like a hamster on a wheel sting my thoughts and I start to feel slightly sick.

A wave of denial hits me. How could Sammy's confession just now be possible? Back then, I spent weeks hunting the truth and there was no evidence to suggest that anything from that wicked night in the phone actually happened. I knew I should have contacted the people at Socialise. I've spent years convincing myself it was all a dream but now I no longer feel sure of anything as the years of rationalising the evil events had taken a mighty blow.

There must be another explanation to explain Sammy's confession. Maybe we did have the conversation in real life and I blocked it out, because it was too traumatic. You do hear of that. It took so much self-persuasion to force myself to believe that the phone trap was a devious dream. I did such a good job convincing myself that the delusion was triggered by my phone obsession. There is now a desperate backtracking task I must endure. I've secured lots of evidence over the years that disproves anything strange happened ten years ago; and I need to confirm again that it all stacks up.

I reach out for my phone. Even though I've been working quite normally with these devices for years now, I can't help but look at it like a bomb that is about to go off as I start to question again if it can trap or even harm me. My mind cries out that I should chuck the damn thing out the window and stay away from phones for the rest of my life. The rational side of me, however, pleads for me to stop acting crazy and demands that I find answers to prove this. Ironically checking through the phone is the only way to do it. I remind myself that I'm fine and there is absolutely no way that a phone can entrap me, before I hunt for evidence of normality.

I find myself searching for the artist Rohnan, who had been off the scene for about five years now. When nothing immediately presents itself about the charity gig story that both inspired me to help others but also terrified me because of the whole experience of reading it inside my phone, I decide to refine the search some more. The date of the trauma was well and truly etched in my mind and I add this to the search term.

I scroll through the results and can't see anything. Then as I scroll back to the top, there it is, as clear as day; the first result in the listing. 'Rohnan confirms Comic Relief gig'. I don't even need to click on the article to know it was the exact same one, from the exact same source.

An angry drop of vomit etches up my throat as I continue to press on and browse further dates which talk about how the gig was to be cancelled and how Rohnan would be making a private charitable donation instead.

Now what about the live video of the party? Was it simply deleted? Did Becky lie through her teeth so I would get off her case? A knot invaded my stomach as it then occurred to me live videos did not actually remain traceable online after 24 hours. They typically disappeared after that time. I think deep down this fact was like a slow-growing tumour in my brain, slowly corrupting the cells and waiting for the kill. There was further trauma. It now seems more than a coincidence that Becky and Jade no longer saw eye to eye after that party. Don't get me wrong, both were the kind of bitches to fall out over nothing, but this occurrence offered very convenient timing. Also, the fact Brad and Jade did get together, seems so much more suspicious and petrifying now.

My head is overwhelmed with ill thoughts. I had seen and heard more than enough for one day. I couldn't handle what was being unearthed. It feels as though my phone is a ticking bomb that could go off at any moment. I'm gripped with a pressing urge to launch the thing out of the car, making sure I leave as much distance between me and the evil machine as I could achieve. I can feel my mind going into meltdown. I order myself to keep calm.

I sit and take a few deep breaths, and as I do, a blinding ray of sun powers through a gaping hole in the stormy sky. I let the warmth shower me for a moment and I immediately feel more relaxed. It swiftly occurs to me that I am in fact here in this moment, unharmed and ready to hopefully change the world; and essentially this was all because of that ominous day. I don't know how I got turned into a phone puppet on that day and I don't know why. Even though this sudden occurrence of horrifying evidence is unbelievably chilling, it still doesn't prove that my memories of what happened are right. I give more thought to the possibility that I could have blocked out trauma from my mind. Maybe I had a mental breakdown that night and this warped my experience of things? Whatever happened, there is nothing I can do about it now. All I can do it focus on the here and now.

I remind myself that I'm a strong, sane and successful business woman and with this, a surge of power embraces me. I've come a long way from that moody and confused teenager who thought everyone was out to get her. It feels like I had been given an almighty test from God and had passed. At this point I also reminded myself that I actually helped to save a man's life after the events that occurred. A feeling of pride helped to suppress my fear. No more worrying and hiding away from the past. I am the master of my own destiny and leave my car with purpose as I stride towards my office for an afternoon which will begin a journey where I can change the world for the better.

It is a short walk to my office, but I'm grateful for it as I let the fresh air continue to clear my mind. I enter the access code to the building and then bounce past reception to where the seeds of my success are being watered. I greet Tom, my young receptionist, with a good afternoon and a determined smile en route before bounding up the stairs towards our meeting room. He offers me a slight look of bemusement at my haste. I don't blame him to be honest as my emotions are all over the place and it must show.

My stylish open-plan office is light in the mid-afternoon sun that has just poked through and I have five staff members all glued to their screens, focussed on building the dream. There is plenty of empty spaces amongst them and if all goes well today (and with the app launch more importantly), I hope to get these filled. I offer everyone a frenzied greeting which is met with confused laughter. I swear they all think I'm a bit barmy and maybe they're right.

I don't stop to chat and head straight to my meeting room which is already occupied with two of the country's finest developers, I had hired to complete my latest and most ambitious project. They all look slightly on edge but relieved as I walk through the door.

'Good afternoon guys, sorry I missed your call Mark.'

A slim guy in his early 30s with a well-groomed beard gives me a weak smile that suggests that it wasn't ok, but thank God you're here.

'Don't worry Lindsey, shall we get straight to it?'

A slight look at my watch confirms that I am almost an hour late and I am all too aware that time is most certainly money with these guys.

My almighty omega moment starts to take a plunge as I try to focus on the task at hand. I know exactly what we are trying to achieve here, but now any thoughts of toying with technology still seem terrifying. I know that I'm physically in the room with those who do the devil's work, but mentally I'm all at sea again. I find myself responding in autopilot.

'Yes, sure, let's do it. I'm really excited to see what you've got for me.'

The two guys look to be appeased by my charm and enthusiasm for their work, their egos calmed by the compliment.

'Great. Well, let's get going,' replies Mark.

At this point, I find myself staring out of the window and notice a small bird perched in a baby pink, cherry blossom tree. It looked peaceful; behind this is a world of neat office buildings, clusters of green, more pink trees, and rolling hills in the distance. This is a world away from screen-glare and my nightmare of phone imprisonment.

I fight to maintain my attention as a fresh-faced and smartly-dressed guy called Darren opens his high-end laptop and starts typing viciously.

'Just need to tweak one final bit of code so we can run in demo mode,' he says.

After a few moments of what could be regarded as awkward silence to those who weren't aware of the tangible anticipation, Darren was done.

'Right, let's get this show on the road. Your nagging voice of reason is ready to guide the way on healthy phone use,' announces Darren with pride, who had clearly been dying to say this line.

'Now, how do you want to work it?' questions Mark.

After a few moments of contemplation, I decide to let them lead the way.

'What do you suggest?'

Looking pleased at having a free reign, Mark responds, 'Why don't we talk you through some of the key features of functionality and then you could have a go at sending out some test invites and then have a go for yourself? After this, we can answer any questions you might have?'

'Sounds great,' I respond.

Evidently smug about my positive reaction, the two guys bounce between each other like a deadly duo, both feeding off each other's self-pride. I switch on the large projector screen in the middle of the meeting room and Darren busies himself, connecting his device to the screen via Bluetooth. He may only be in his early 20s but Darren clearly seems to be the one with most technical attributes. I sit there in bewilderment as he rattles off explanations about the various plug-ins, potential bug-fixes that would come with new versions and script that went into creating different areas of app functionality. I watched in wonder as the various elements of the app were spoon-fed to me through the PC-friendly pages shown on the screen.

Aside from the complexities, it sounds and looks positive. I can finally see that my vision has been achieved and it looks to be on the cusp of being unleashed to the public. The results so far have gone beyond my expectations and I get a giddy sense that we are about to make our mark on the world.

There is an option to create a personalised mentor, a built-in phone usage tracker and automatic prompt when the user's set phone usage time is being exceeded. You could also set yourself goals, usage restrictions and plans. There are also videos which offer insights into the importance of real social interaction and the danger of too much phone time.

I'm literally swelling with excitement and pride at finally seeing my ideas get centre stage and for the first time all day, I start to relax a little.

'Ok, so you've got all of that?' Mark asks. Excited by what I've heard so far, and also relieved to be reaching a successful conclusion, I respond with enthusiasm once more.

'Yes, this all sounds great Mark. What happens now, can I have a play around on the software so I can really sink my teeth into what we'll have to offer?'

Mark offers me a mischievous looking-smirk and replies, 'I knew you would love what we had to offer and of course we can get onto having a good play around with the app, but all in good time.'

I hadn't actually met Mark in person before now and even though he looks to have delivered everything I had dreamed of, there is something in his demeanour I don't like. He seems very smug and he is giving off an air of arrogance. I've become used to this already in the world of business and I assume most developers are like this.

Mark then continues with a giant bombshell which shatters my recent feeling of contentment. 'Well there's actually one final trick up our sleeves that I think you are going to love.'

Mark is grinning like a Cheshire cat as he builds up the suspense. This revelation certainly catches me off guard. Darren also grins with enthusiasm as he awaits the announcement.

'Oh right, what it is?' I enquire with anxious curiosity. I was startled by the sudden air of suspense, when it looked as though the cards were already dealt.

'Ok, well, basically it's an install we can include for those who have VR compatibility, whereby they can experience all of the features we offer in full VR.'

'All they need to do is wirelessly connect their phone to the VR and they cannot only navigate our app but also their phone by using finger movements alone.'

Not for the first time today, I find myself strangled in thought. A hamster starts a constant wheel sprint in my stomach as a very real sense of danger is being stewed in this room. Five minutes ago, I thought my experience was a warning to help prevent an abomination on this earth, however now I start to think it is an invitation towards it. A surge of terrifying paranoia grips me and I develop an instant and great mistrust towards the developers. I must keep cool, dig deeper into the detail of this function and stop this from happening if need be.

I can tell Mark is pining to receive the praise he believes is justified; however, it is Darren who responds in an effort to claw things back.

'Of course, the software is not yet complete, we still have a few bugs to contend with just at the moment, but we do have a working demo that we can show you that we think you will be impressed with.'

I know I must see for myself the carnival of chaos that is being conjured up in this very room. At this point, I just hope I have the power to steer the ship back towards a non-lethal goal. Something tells me that I can't trust these crooks to show me everything I need to see. I must examine the ins and outs of the VR function for myself. If I don't like what I see, I may have no choice but to pull the plug on the whole operation.

'Yeah, interesting idea,' I respond in delay.

I can see from the expression in both men's eyes that this is not the reaction they were banking on. They look at each other in confusion. I'm determined to throw them off their ambition to sell me this poison until I see it for myself.

'It sounds very exciting,' I reply without sincerity this time. 'But would it be possible for me to have a good play around on the demo you gents have put together for the regular features before we delve into it?' I question with purpose.

The two men look wounded by my fractious behaviour and simply stare at me in bemusement.

'In fact, have you both had any lunch yet?' I continue, desperate for an excuse to get them out of the room for a while so I can see for myself what I'm dealing with.

Once again, I am met with a mutual look of concern.

'No, not yet, we were going to grab something after the meeting,' says Mark. 'To be honest, Lindsey, ideally, we were hoping to give you a full introduction and overview of the concept first. I can assure you that the technology fits the brief in terms of the vision and goals you are trying to achieve.'

Mark clearly senses my unease and is frantically trying to get me back on board. I have to think carefully in order to convince them otherwise.

'I completely understand, of course,' I assure. 'It's just I want to quickly satisfy myself that everything on the brief is covered so far and that it makes sense in my own mind before we get too immersed in what I'm sure is a fab bit of tech. Why don't you go and grab a bite now while I quickly try and get a basic grip with how it all works? Please tell me to shut-up and carry on if you think it is for the greater good, no problem at all. I just think it will be best for my understanding to get hands-on as we go along. Your call.'

Darren gives a perplexed but enquiring look at Mark to see what his thoughts are. He does not look overly-convinced at my capability to work through the demo alone but agrees anyway. I think my little ego-boosting compliment about the tech helped get the men on side.

'Well, to be fair, it is your call, Lindsey; it is, after all, your project at the end of the day. By all means, have a play around. I should warn you though, a few things might not quite make sense at this stage without our walkthrough, but if you get stuck at all with anything, just video call me and I'll talk you through it. We can of course go through things in more detail after lunch,' Mark says, clearly as a backup for when I inevitably become stuck. He then hands over a tablet device which is presumably preloaded with the demo app also.

'Yeah, sure, no problem,' I respond more enthusiastically then I feel, as I snatch it from him.

'Ok, you simply click on demo mode and then follow the prompts to the different features that will automatically appear,' Mark instructs.

'As mentioned, the VR functionality isn't quite ready yet, but the demo pretty much is if you wanted to check it out?'

I have every intention of reviewing the VR content but play it cool: 'Ok sure, I might as well see what it is all about. I'm sure I will get the gist of it all.'

'Ok, great,' replies Mark, and with that the developers swiftly leave the room and me alone with the tablet, which features the dummy app name of 'The Over-Tech Tracker' displayed in turquoise letters across the screen.

It feels like I am able to breathe again slightly as the men leave; however, it quickly dawns on me what wicked potential lies innocently on the table beside me. I know I must review the content, but for a few minutes I remain glued to my seat, frozen with the fear of playing around with technology once more.

I know I must keep it together; I know I have to be strong. For years, I have been toying with technology for the greater good and I know this deadly duel to find out if the developers have added content that goes against the goal for safe phone use, needs to be done. In their goal for technologic advancement, I don't think all innovators consider the potential for harm on the consumer. I will be damned if something happens which unintentionally defeats the purpose of what I'm trying to achieve here. After the disturbing revelations from my meeting with Sammy earlier, my task to make sure everything is kosher, seems even more urgent right now.

I must remind myself though that whatever these guys were working on, it absolutely is not the same as what I endured. It requires a headset, for God's sake. Besides, it isn't even ready, I convince myself.

Then another grave thought occurs to me. None of the guys mentioned anything about a headset. Headsets are always needed for the VR experience and yet no mention of one. I look around the room where the guys were sat and see no evidence of any being left for demonstration. It must have just slipped their minds I assure myself. I did usher them out the room rather promptly. Regardless of my rising fear, I know I have the power to unearth and potentially stop all of this. The app is already open on the screen as I awaken the tablet. I press the big demo button in the middle of the display and pray that nothing untoward happens. It doesn't. Why would it? I am instead prompted to create a buddy, of which I decide to skip and create later. I am instead given what looks like a self-start avatar which was a cartoon teenage girl, dressed in ripped jeans, a plain white T-shirt and a blonde ponytail.

I must admit I like the simplicity and connotations of normality here. I could praise the developers for that. The girl who introduces herself as Lexi points me towards the menu in the left-hand corner of the screen which prompts a drop down with lots of options, including: Monitor, Plan, Restrict, Goals, Achievements, Videos, Rewards and Immerse. I spend some time navigating through each one and am pleasantly surprised at their ease of use.

I'm shown by my 'temporary buddy' how to make various plans at different periods of time based on what suited me. I'm also introduced to a hub of my own videos of people who are talking about their own experiences of being hooked on their phones all the time, which makes me swell with pride.

As Lexi guides me through each step, something about the emoji character seems very familiar and fills me with dread. After her demo I change my mind about the 'create a buddy' option and find myself hunting down the source of this character and come across a title in the settings called 'My Buddy'. I click on it. Lexi appears as an editable character that I can rotate and edit in great detail. I can change her name, clothes, facial features along with a whole host of other character attributes. I notice a swipe-across option which leads me on to other pre-created characters.

The wretched stomach knot from earlier, tightens.

I swipe through a multitude of different characters of different gender and race. Some are athletic, some are not. Short, tall, young, old, you name it, the developers had thought of it. I had to admire their attention to detail.

Just as the panic starts to ease off, a bolt of lightning strikes me. I stop swiping as I discover the horror, I was hoping I would never find. There she is; the emoji figure that has haunted me for years. She is identical to the girl who popped into my nightmare that fateful night when I was sixteen. Her name, 'Jemma', shone blindingly above her ominous looking being.

This is beyond impossible. I must be experiencing another delusion. Every ounce of my being tells me I should close down the app in case this is real. My gut feeling was right. I need to shut down this whole operation, before it's too late. Another urge, deep down inside however, propels me to go on. Something tells me that my experience from that fateful night isn't over just yet and it is my duty to slay the dragon in case this curse somehow plagues the earth despite my efforts to halt the developers.

I wince at Jemma with fear. She is wearing the same outfit as when we last met. The weird sandals and baggie dungarees no longer look bizarre as they once did. The realisation that this is now the fashion, blows my mind.

The ghost from my past just stands there, hand on waist casually swaying slightly. She sports a neutral expression and says nothing to me. There is an option on screen to select this emoji as my guide. I must be beyond crazy, but I choose to select her. I am immediately reacquainted with that OTT grin she gave me all those years ago.

'Hi there, my name is Jemma. Nice to meet you, Lindsey,' she says.

Interesting introduction. I feel slightly relieved that she doesn't recognise me or acknowledge me as though we've already met. She knows my name, but that doesn't mean anything, as the app would be set up with my details inputted already, I would assume.

'I am here to help you think about how you can get the most out of using your phone in a healthy way, if that sounds like a plan?' she continues.

A little bubble in the corner of the screen prompts me to talk back.

'Ok, let's do it,' I reply.

'That's great. I can see that you have already had a tour of; Monitor, Plan, Restrict, Goals, Achievements, Videos, Rewards. Would you like me to take you through the 'Immersion' option?' she asks.

It dawns on me that Jemma must be talking about the VR function. The realisation and request leave me shaking with fear. All those years ago, it was a virtual reality that I found myself enslaved in. Until earlier this day, I thought I had been punished with the mother of all nightmares. Now it seems as though my unworldly experience was something else entirely. Am I about to unleash something similar, worse even, on the world?

I take a deep breath and then respond like I've been asked

to cut a wire to defuse a bomb.

'Ok then.'

Jemma beams again and it is a terrifying look.

'No problem at all,' she complies.

Jemma clicks her finger, the screen changes but the result is a bit anti-climax. I just get some plain black text which reads, you are in manager mode. Jemma must be showing me this as an administrative feature. I find this weird. Below the text is an edit button, which I instinctively press in the absence of any other options.

Next, I am greeted with an option that says, 'Click to edit module title', which appears to be an editable heading for the entire Immersion software. This instinctively leads me to press once more without any further prompt from Jemma to do so. There is a sudden switch from me being shown what to do, to taking control of the app's destiny. I don't need to follow the dictations of a fictitious being and I find my brain is working in auto-pilot as I start typing the only logical title for the part of the app I can think of: 'Virtuality.'

I am then enticed on screen to invite participants, in which my name is ominously the only one already automatically selected. I put a tick next to it. At this point, I am losing cognitive thought once more, but I no longer feel in danger. All thoughts of Jemma melt away at this point.

The next command says, 'Please select schedule date,' but again this is already set. It is impossibly set for a date in the past. The date holds all the significance in the world, 18.03.2015, the exact day I had been invited to a world of virtual reality. Scarier still it asks me to set a specific time. Incredibly the digits 9.31am are already glaring at me.

It is only now in fact that things really do become clear. There is no longer a need for fear, just one more action to take. I press 'Send Invitation'.

At this exact moment, ten years earlier, Lindsey Hoodwink finds herself bored in her maths class. Her school blazer pocket vibrates violently, and her smartphone waits patiently for what is yet to come. She has created her own nightmare.

ABOUT THE AUTHOR

This is my first novel and it is one that I didn't mean to make. In the beginning I had another pressing idea mapped out in my head, until one seemingly random family visit changed all that.

Given the dark themes portrayed within my story I don't think it would be right to shed light on exactly where my inspiration came from. What I would say is that something clicked in my head that night and made me realise the powerful and potentially harmful pull that smartphones and social media can have on us. In that moment a concept for The Invite was born.

Interestingly this novel actually began life as a short story, but it quickly became clear that it had the potential to offer more. During the planning stage, the ideas kept on coming and I knew I needed to take you on a deeper and darker journey in order to really hammer my message home.

Moments of disturbing fantasy that have featured throughout The Invite have been inspired by the grave problems many of us experience with smartphone addiction. Lindsey's made-up journey aims to reflect the real-life ability of our own devices to play us like a yo-yo, toying with our emotions, whilst making us constantly crave for more. When I look at how things have changed in the past 10 years in terms of our relationship with rapidly advancing smart devices, it is scary to think about where we are heading in say another 10 years' time.

Already I can see people spiralling ever deeper into unhealthy habits with their phones (myself included). This is why I knew I needed to offer all my energy to this project and see it through to the end asap.

Then the truly horrible COVID-19 pandemic happened and it gave me a rare opportunity to one, offer temporary escape from the suffering going on around the world and two, crack on writing without distraction. In a strange way it felt like I had been gifted a chance to fulfil my duty to deliver something important to the world. I sincerely hope I have managed to fulfil that goal.

I don't think technology is necessarily the devil and our downfall though. On the other hand, I think it has incredible power that needs to be exercised with caution. If The Invite offers just a bit of that caution, I can say I've set out what I aimed to achieve.

Now that I'm done, my patient brain is free to finally run riot with my original novel idea. In fact, I have already started to revisit my old plans as part of my next project, which has been a long time in waiting.

To join in the conversation about Lindsey's nightmare or find out more about my latest writing pursuits, feel free to check out my social media pages and blog.

Facebook @authorcpriches
Twitter @CPRiches1
Wordpress criches90.wordpress.com
Instagram @authorcpriches1

Printed in Great Britain
by Amazon

82457369R10077